MEET THE FO

Fortune of the Month: Gavin Fortunado

Age: 30

Vital Statistics: Simply irresistible.

Claim to Fame: This golden boy is a successful corporate attorney and the son of real estate mogul Kenneth Fortunado—and a bona fide Fortune to boot.

Romantic Prospects: Fantastic—just don't ask him to commit. He recently convinced family friend and Fortunado Real Estate employee Christine Briscoe to be his temporary pretend girlfriend just to get his parents off his back. He's too busy having fun to worry about marriage. Why is everyone so darned eager to see him settle down?

"This whole thing was a lark. Christine was going to be my 'girl' for just a few weeks while I was in Austin. It's funny how easy it was to convince everyone we were a couple. She's not the kind of woman I usually date.

"Why can't we just be allowed to have fun? Why does everything have to have a label? *And why can't I stop thinking about her?*"

* * *

THE FORTUNES OF TEXAS:
THE LOST FORTUNES
Family secrets revealed!

Dear Reader,

I'm so excited to be part of The Fortunes of Texas series this year and to be kicking off 2019 with *A Deal Made in Texas*.

Fake-engagement stories are some of my favorites to read and to write. I love the push and pull when characters discover that their pretend relationship is resulting in real emotions.

Gavin Fortunado is definitely a catch—he's handsome, successful and charming. He's also used to taking the easy way out when it comes to truly giving his heart. Until he makes the deal of a lifetime with Christine Briscoe. A fake relationship with an old friend seems like a simple plan for distracting his well-meaning family from his love life. And Christine can't resist the chance to spend time with Gavin, who has been her secret crush for years. But when their feelings for each other become all too real, Gavin has to decide how far he'll go to win her heart.

I hope you enjoy reading their story as much as I loved writing it.

Please come say hi on Facebook (Facebook.com/michellemajorbooks) or at michellemajor.com.

Happy reading!

Michelle

A Deal
Made in Texas

—

Michelle Major

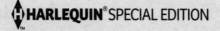
HARLEQUIN® SPECIAL EDITION

Special thanks and acknowledgment are given to
Michelle Major for her contribution to
The Fortunes of Texas: The Lost Fortunes miniseries.

Recycling programs
for this product may
not exist in your area.

ISBN-13: 978-1-335-57358-2

A Deal Made in Texas

HARLEQUIN®
™ www.Harlequin.com

Printed in U.S.A.

Michelle Major grew up in Ohio but dreamed of living in the mountains. Soon after graduating with a degree in journalism, she pointed her car west and settled in Colorado. Her life and house are filled with one great husband, two beautiful kids, a few furry pets and several well-behaved reptiles. She's grateful to have found her passion writing stories with happy endings. Michelle loves to hear from her readers at michellemajor.com.

Visit the Author Profile page
at Harlequin.com for more titles.

To the Fortunes of Texas team of editors—
thank you for helping me make this story shine.

Chapter One

"I love weddings."

Gavin Fortunado glanced at his sister Schuyler, who stood next to him in the ballroom of the Driskill Hotel in downtown Austin, her long blond hair pulled into an elaborate braided updo. The understated opulence and elegant decor of the historic venue only made the starched collar of the tuxedo he wore feel even stuffier.

"I know you do." Gavin drained the glass of bubbly champagne he'd raised after his father's toast to another sister, Maddie, and her new husband, Zach McCarter. The fizzy liquid churned in his stomach, and he looked toward the crowded bar, mentally calculating how long it would take to get to the front of the line and order a whiskey neat. He had a feeling he'd need something more substantial than champagne to make it through this evening.

He placed his empty glass on a nearby table as Schuyler wrapped her elegant fingers around his arm. "Maddie is a beautiful bride," she said as she leaned against him, dabbing at the corner of one eye with her free hand.

"Yep." He patted his sister's hand. "You were, too." Schuyler had married Carlo Mendoza, vice president of Mendoza Winery, last spring in the sculpture garden at the winery in the Texas Hill Country outside the city. Just as he had this weekend, Gavin had flown in from Denver for Schuyler's big day. He loved his three sisters and appreciated that two of them, who were now married, had picked great guys. He liked and respected both of his brothers-in-law. Any guy who was man enough to take on Schuyler or Maddie was definitely ready to join the family.

Speaking of Schuyler's husband, where was Carlo now? Gavin could use a diversion before Schuyler started in on him.

Too late.

"I'm sure you'll find a beautiful bride, as well." Schuyler gave his arm a squeeze. The touch was gentle, but somehow Gavin felt like an animal caught in a steel trap. Sweat beaded between his shoulder blades and rolled down his back. He groaned inwardly as he noticed the line at the bar had gotten longer.

"You did a great job with all the wedding planning," he said, ignoring his sister's comment. "I know Maddie appreciated it since she's so wrapped up in the Fortunado Real Estate Austin office right now. I don't know how you convinced Mom to allow another wedding to take place here instead of in Houston. I thought she'd pressure Maddie and Zach to get married closer to home."

"It's only a couple hours' drive from Mom and Dad's house, but Maddie couldn't spare any extra time. She and Zach are burning the real estate candle at both ends these days."

Gavin loved all his sisters and brothers, but he and Maddie were only nine months apart in age, so they'd always been especially close. Her relationship with Zach had gotten off to a rocky start last year, as both of them had been vying to be named the new president of Fortunado Real Estate, the company Kenneth Fortunado had founded and devoted his life to for years.

Of the six Fortunado children, Maddie was the one most invested in the family business, although the baby of the family, Valene, was quickly coming into her own as a real estate agent. Their oldest brother, Everett, was a successful doctor. Connor worked as an executive at a corporate search firm in Denver so Gavin hung out with him on a regular basis. Ever since coming to Austin last year, Schuyler had joined the staff of the Mendoza Winery, heading up branding for the company. Gavin had spent his entire career with a corporate law firm headquartered in Denver. He knew his parents were proud of all of them, but Maddie had the same passion for real estate as Kenneth, and she'd gone toe-to-toe with Zach until they'd fallen in love.

It made Gavin smile to see his practical, pragmatic sister head over heels, especially since Zach was the perfect partner for her, as driven and dedicated to the business as Maddie.

"Maybe you'll be the one to tie the knot in Houston," Schuyler suggested cheerily. "I could see it at—"

"Stop." Gavin managed to extricate himself from his sister's grip without having to resort to chewing off his own arm. "I'm not getting married. What is it with everyone and this obsession with weddings? Mom and Dad have been dropping not-so-subtle hints since I stepped off the plane."

Schuyler sighed. "We want you to be happy."

"I *am* happy," Gavin insisted.

She arched one delicate brow in response. "You could be *really* happy."

Gavin rolled his eyes. He wasn't about to get into an argument about his level of contentment. Of course he was happy. Why wouldn't he be? He had a great job working with a prestigious law firm and was on track to be named partner within a year. He owned a fantastic loft in the bustling Lower Downtown neighborhood. The city was a perfect mix of urban and outdoorsy, with enough cowboy left to appeal to his Texas heart. Plus, Colorado offered almost limitless opportunities for the adrenaline-pumping adventures Gavin couldn't seem to get enough of during his downtime. He rock-climbed, mountain-biked and skied every weekend throughout the winter. Well, not this January weekend since he was at his sister's wedding, being subjected to the third degree by his well-intentioned family.

"Look at Everett," Schuyler continued, pointing across the room to where their brother stood talking to a friend of their parents'. His wife, Lila, was at his side, Everett's hand on her back. "He's happy."

As if on cue, Everett glanced down at Lila, and the

tenderness in his gaze made Gavin's chest ache the tiniest bit. Lila smiled up at him, practically glowing, and he drew her in closer. Gavin studied the couple, high school sweethearts who'd reunited last spring after years apart. There was something different about them tonight, a new kind of energy to their already strong connection.

Schuyler nudged him, drawing his attention back to her. "Don't you want a woman to look at you like that?"

"What I want is a drink," he told her. "And for you to drop the subject of my love life."

"When was the last time you had a serious girlfriend?"

Never, Gavin thought to himself. He only dated women who wanted the same things he did: fun, adventure and a good time. "Would you like a glass of wine?"

"You didn't answer my question." Schuyler placed her hands on her slim hips. As Maddie's matron of honor, she wore a burgundy-colored cocktail dress and matching heels that gave her a few extra inches of height. At six feet two inches tall, Gavin still towered over his petite sister. Her classic features and tiny frame made her look like any other beautiful young woman, but Gavin knew underneath the subtle makeup and coiffed hair beat the heart of a tenacious fighter. Once Schuyler latched on to a cause, she gave "dog with a bone" new meaning. It had been that determination that had led the Fortunados to the discovery that they were actually part of the famous Fortune family.

Schuyler loved a challenge and a quest, and Gavin didn't relish being her next one.

"Who says I don't have a serious girlfriend?" he

countered, willing to say just about anything to make her drop the subject. "Maybe I just didn't want to subject her to my crazy family."

"I don't believe you."

"Doesn't make it less true. If you all weren't such true-love tyrants, I would have told you about it before." Gavin smiled to himself. That should be enough to keep her occupied for a while.

He realized his mistake as her eyes lit with excitement. "Who is she? How long have you been dating? Why didn't you bring her to the wedding?"

"I'm heading to the bar," he said, invoking his big-brother selective hearing. "I'll get you a glass of Chardonnay. Oh, and it looks like Maddie is having trouble with her train. You have work to do, sis."

"Gavin, I want to hear about your lady."

"Maddie needs you. Gotta go." He moved around her, dodging like he was back on the high school football team when she reached for him.

"Valene can help. Wait... Gavin."

He waved over his shoulder and called, "Back in a sec," having no intention of returning to his sister. She'd regroup soon enough, anyway. Another glance over his shoulder showed Schuyler following him.

He tugged at his collar and glanced around, catching the eye of the slim redhead standing near the corner of the bar. Not exactly catching her eye, as he got the impression that she'd been watching him approach. Either way, she was a friendly face and he'd take it.

"Christine," he called, not daring to check on Schuyler's approach. He wrapped an arm around Christine Briscoe's shoulders. "Great to see you. How have you been? You look lovely. Shall we dance?"

"Um..." Christine, who'd worked for his father's real estate agency in Houston for close to a decade, seemed at a loss for words. That was fine. Gavin didn't need her to speak. As long as she came with him.

The man standing next to her, average height with dark hair and the start of a paunch that indicated he'd done too many keg stands back in college, frowned and made to step forward. Gavin took an immediate dislike to the guy but flashed a grin and held up one finger. "You don't mind if I steal Christine for a dance, right?"

He didn't wait for an answer. He grabbed Christine's hand—soft skin and fine-boned, he noticed—and tugged her toward the dance floor, breathing a sigh of relief as he saw that Schuyler had been waylaid by a distant cousin on their mother's side of the family.

The music changed from an up-tempo dance number to a slow ballad. Automatically, he wrapped his arms around Christine's waist, careful to be respectful of her personal space since he'd basically hijacked her for this dance.

She lifted her hands to his shoulders and glanced up at him.

"Hi, there," he said with his most charming smile.

"Hi," she breathed. "You, too. Well. Thanks. Yes."

He felt his mouth drop open and closed it again. "I think I missed part of the conversation."

She tugged her bottom lip between her teeth and his mouth went dry. He'd known Christine for years, but how had he never noticed the way her mouth was shaped like a perfect Cupid's bow, the lower lip slightly fuller and damned kissable, if he had the inclination?

Which he didn't. He couldn't. She was a cover to save him from his sister's meddling in his private life.

Clearly, Schuyler had messed with his head because he'd never thought of Christine as anything more than a casual friend before this moment—never gave her much thought at all if he had to admit the truth.

"I'm responding to your comments," she answered, somewhat primly. "It's great to see you, too. I'm well. Thanks for the compliment. Yes, I'd like to dance."

"Ah." He felt one side of his mouth curve. This time the smile was natural. Why did it feel so unfamiliar? "You're precise."

She frowned. "Oh, you weren't looking for a response? The questions were rhetorical." Color flooded her cheeks and it fascinated him to watch the freckles that dotted her skin almost disappear against the blush. "I should have figured."

"No... I..." He shook his head. "I'm a little bit off my game tonight."

"Your game," she murmured.

"Not that this is a game," he amended quickly. "It's a wedding."

"Your *sister's* wedding," Christine agreed, sounding amused.

"The Fortunados are dropping like flies," he said, glancing around for Schuyler, whom he thankfully didn't see in the vicinity. "Schuyler seems to think I'm next. Can you keep a secret?"

Christine nodded solemnly.

"I told her I have a girlfriend."

"But you don't?"

"No, and that's how I like it." He pulled her closer to avoid a couple trying some sort of complicated spin and tried not to notice the feel of her soft curves pressing against the front of his tux. This dance was about avoiding Schuyler. Nothing more. "For some reason, my sister can't seem to accept that. It was easier to lie, although I'm not sure she believed me."

"I'm sure you could find a girlfriend if you wanted one."

He grimaced. "But I don't want one. Not even a little bit."

"Oh."

He had the strange sensation that he'd disappointed her and didn't like the feeling.

"How's Denver?" Christine asked quietly after a moment of awkward silence between them.

"Good," he answered and struggled to come up with something better to say. Something interesting. Charming. Gavin was well-known for his charm. He had an easy way with women that made him popular, even with his ex-girlfriends. Where was that legendary charm now?

He couldn't figure out what the hell was wrong with him. Had he allowed Schuyler to rattle him that much? Hell, he came from a family of six kids. Good-natured teasing was nothing new.

"Did you cut your ski trip short to come to the wedding?"

He blinked. "I did, actually. How did you know?"

"Your sisters talk about you a lot," she said. She stiffened in his arms, making him regret questioning her. He liked dancing with Christine. She was just the right height and her body fit against his perfectly. She smelled clean and fresh, like strawberries or springtime or sunshine. Okay, that was stupid. Sunshine didn't have a scent.

He needed to get a hold of himself, but all he could

manage was hoping she'd relax into him again. The song ended and another ballad began. Gavin would have to tip the bandleader later for his sense of timing.

"Do you ski?" he asked, tightening his hold on her ever so slightly, splaying his hand across her lower back.

She laughed, low and husky, and his stomach flipped wildly. He hadn't expected that kind of laugh from strait-laced Christine Briscoe. "No skiing for me. I've never even been to Colorado."

"You'll have to visit," he told her. The way her eyes widened in shock was like he'd invited her to have wild monkey sex on the hood of his car. The image did crazy things to his breathing, and he pushed it out of his mind.

"Th-things are b-busy," she stammered, "at the office right now."

"That's right. You moved to Austin to manage the new branch. My dad mentioned that."

"I'm originally from Austin, and it was a great opportunity," she confirmed. "Of course, I loved working for your dad in Houston, too."

"Of course." He felt the sensation of someone staring at him and glanced toward the bar. The man Christine had been standing next to was still there, shooting daggers in Gavin's direction.

"Did I steal you from your boyfriend?" Even though it was no business of his, he didn't like the idea of this woman belonging to another man.

She shook her head, her full mouth pursing into a thin line. "Maddie and Zach invited everyone from the Austin office to the wedding. Bobby and I work together, but that's all, despite his best efforts. He's a good real estate agent but can't seem to understand that I'm not interested in dating him. In fact, you kind of rescued me."

"So then I'm your hero?"

Christine blushed again, and Gavin couldn't help but wonder what it would take to make her whole body flush that lovely shade of pink.

"I don't know about that," she murmured, her gaze focused on the knot of his bow tie.

He forced a chuckle, ignoring the pang of disappointment that lanced his chest at her words. What was going on with him tonight? He didn't want or need to be anyone's hero. "Already you know me too well," he said as the song ended.

Her eyes darted to his like she'd been caught with her hand in the cookie jar. "I should get back to…um… the bar." She squeezed shut her eyes then opened them again and offered him a lopsided smile. The first strains of a popular country line dance song started. "I'm not much for this kind of dancing."

"We have that in common," he told her then led her through the crowd. "Thanks for helping me out," he said as they stopped at the end of the bar. At least the guy from earlier was nowhere to be seen. He waited for her to say something, oddly reluctant to have this strange interlude come to an end.

She crossed her arms over her chest and nodded, barely making eye contact. "Enjoy the rest of your night."

"You, too," he said and took a step away, to be almost immediately stopped by an old family friend.

He glanced over his shoulder to see that Christine had already turned toward the bar. She was well and truly done with him.

Gavin didn't have much experience with being blown off by a woman, but he recognized the signs just the same. Christine Briscoe obviously wasn't having the same reaction to him as he was to her. He was more disappointed than he would have imagined.

Chapter Two

Christine picked up the glass of wine the bartender placed in front of her and drained half of it in one long gulp.

She'd just had her heart's desire handed to her on a silver platter and she'd made a mess of the whole thing. Gavin Fortunado might not be a hero, but he'd been her secret crush since the moment she'd set eyes on him almost ten years ago.

For ten years she'd harbored fantasies about her boss's adventurous, drop-dead-gorgeous youngest son. Then tonight, out of nowhere, he'd taken her into his arms, like a scene from every Hallmark movie she'd ever watched. And she loved a good romance.

Unfortunately, Christine hadn't even been able to put together a decent sentence. He'd actually flirted with her. Of course, Gavin flirted with everyone. Not that she knew him well, other than adoring him from afar, but he'd come into the Fortunado Real Estate Agency office in Houston often enough over the years.

She'd watched his easy banter with his sisters as well as the women who worked in the office. He was always charming but respectful and had a knack for remembering names and details. Half the women she knew in Houston had a crush on him, and she imagined it was much the same in Denver.

At first, when his gaze had met hers as he strode toward the bar, she'd thought he might call her out for staring. She'd been trying to ignore Bobby, who seemed to think he was God's gift to women. He was harmless but annoying, and Christine wasn't sure why he wouldn't give up on her. Maybe because she had very little social life to speak of so he assumed she should be grateful for his attention.

Irritated was more like it.

He'd been blathering on about some property he couldn't close, and Christine had been watching Gavin talk to Schuyler. Or rather argue. She was used to seeing Gavin smiling and jovial and hadn't understood the tension that made his broad shoulders appear stiff. Unlike her own, the Fortunado family was tight-knit so it bothered her to see the brother and sister at odds.

She'd been shocked when Gavin had approached the bar and taken her hand. It might have been a simple dance to him. For Christine, having Gavin pull her close, her body pressed against his, was the culmination of all her secret desires come to life. Of all the single women at the reception, he'd picked her. Did that mean something?

Probably not, but a girl could dream. Sadly, all she'd

be left with was her dreams since she'd been so dis-
combobulated that she hadn't been able to truly enjoy
the moment. Or relax. Or hold up her end of the conversation.

What was the point, anyway? Gavin lived life in the
fast lane. She could barely get out of first gear. Normally, her boring routine didn't bother her. She was
good at her job, had a cute apartment and a sweet rescue
dog that adored her. She owned her own car and one designer purse she'd splurged on last year. The barista at
her neighborhood coffee shop sometimes remembered
her order, which never failed to make her feel special.
She had a good life.

Only occasionally did she think about what it would
be like to have more. To be fun and sporty like her sister, Aimee, or confident in the way of the Fortunado
sisters. To be the kind of woman who could attract a
man like Gavin.

She took another drink of wine and turned back toward the reception. The dance floor was filled with wedding guests, all of them laughing and swaying whether
they had rhythm or not. Christine should join the crowd.
Despite her two left feet, she loved to dance. But the
thought of drawing attention to herself made her cheeks
flame. Drat her pale Irish complexion. She had no abil-
ity to hide her feelings when her blush gave them away
every time.

She had a travel-size powder compact in her purse.
Maybe a little freshening of her makeup would help
her feel more confident. Out of the corner of her eye,
she saw Bobby heading in her direction. She grabbed
the glass of wine and slipped into the hallway, turning the corner toward the bathroom, only to find her

way blocked by Gavin and Schuyler. Immediately, she slipped behind a potted palm, curiosity about the Fortunados getting the best of her despite the fact that it was wrong to eavesdrop.

"Come on," Schuyler urged. "At least tell me her name. A name and then I'll leave you alone."

"You don't fool me for a second," Gavin said, amusement and irritation warring in his tone. "I'm not telling you anything."

Schuyler threw up her hands. "Because this mystery woman doesn't exist. Admit it, you aren't dating anyone."

Gavin opened his mouth, but Schuyler held up a finger. "At least not anyone serious."

"Oh, it's serious. It's also none of your business."

"Tell me something about her. One thing, Gavin."

"She has blue eyes," he answered without hesitation then added, "And fiery red hair."

"A ginger." Schuyler rubbed her hands together. "I need more details."

Gavin shook his head. "You said one thing. I gave you two."

"Where did you meet? Why didn't you bring her? How long have you been dating?"

"Schuyler, stop."

"I can't," she admitted with a laugh. "I need a new project now that Maddie's wedding is over. You're it."

"I'm not," Gavin insisted, running a hand through his thick hair.

He looked so uncomfortable and unaccustomedly vulnerable that Christine's heart stuttered. Tonight was the first time she'd seen this side of Gavin. He seemed almost human...not so picture-perfect, and it made her like him all the more. Which was dangerous, because she already liked him way more than was wise.

Without thinking, she took a step forward, away from her spot behind the fake plant. Gavin glanced up for one instant, and he looked so darn happy to see her. She wanted that look in his eyes to last. So instead of retreating, as her brain instructed, she moved toward them.

Schuyler glanced over her shoulder. "Hey, Christine. Are you having fun?"

Christine swallowed against the ball of nerves stuck in her throat. "It was a beautiful wedding, and Maddie and Zach look really happy. You did an amazing job with the planning."

"Thanks." Schuyler's smile was so genuine, Christine almost let the conversation end there. She was an honest person who valued her job and the relationships she'd forged with each of the Fortunados. But dancing with Gavin had been like eating a bite of cake after dieting for years. One taste wasn't nearly enough. She wanted the whole piece. "Please don't be upset with Gavin," she said, working hard to ensure her voice didn't waver.

Schuyler frowned. "Do you mean our argument out here?" She laughed softly. "Don't worry. It's a friendly brother and sister thing. I have to convince him to give up the name of the woman—"

"I asked him not to say anything." Christine wrapped an arm around Gavin's waist and leaned in close. "I wasn't sure if your dad would approve of us." She glanced up at Gavin and smiled. He was staring at her like she'd just sprouted a second head. Not exactly catching on to her plan, which made sense because she didn't actually have one.

"Wait." Schuyler gasped, her gaze ricocheting between the two of them. "What?"

Christine looked at Schuyler once more. "I hope you can understand…we wanted to keep things private. It was never my intention to deceive you, but—"

"Are you saying that you're Gavin's ghost girlfriend?"

"I know it probably comes as a surprise."

"Understatement of the century," Schuyler muttered. "You can't expect me to believe—"

"It doesn't matter what you believe." Gavin looped an arm around Christine, dropping a kiss on the top of her head that she felt all the way to her toes. "Christine isn't a ghost, but think about how you were giving me the third degree. I didn't want her to have to deal with that, not when I wasn't here to protect her."

Christine resisted the urge to whimper. Maybe it was the wine, but the thought of Gavin protecting her made funny things happen to her insides.

Schuyler's mouth dropped open. She stared at them for several long seconds. Christine tried to act normal and not like she might spontaneously combust at any moment. She rested her head against Gavin's chest, and as great as dancing with him had been, this took things to a new level. Without having to concentrate on the steps, she could enjoy his warmth and the feel of his rock-solid muscle. Not to mention the way he smelled, a mix of expensive cologne and soap. Would it be weird if she reached up on tiptoe, buried her face against his neck and just sniffed? Yeah, definitely weird.

She waited for Schuyler to call them out on the lie.

No way would anyone, let alone Gavin's perceptive sister, believe that they were a couple.

"Well…okay, then," Schuyler said slowly. "I'll admit I'm at a loss for words."

"Thank heavens for small favors," Gavin muttered.

"I still can't believe… I mean how long have you two been an item?"

"A while," Gavin said before Christine could answer. A good thing, too, because the reality of what she'd done was suddenly crashing over her.

"Don't tell your dad," she blurted, earning a frown from Schuyler and a gentle squeeze from Gavin.

"He loves you like you're part of the family," Schuyler told her. "You know that."

"He loves me *working* for the family," Christine clarified. "This is different."

"Gavin, tell her she has nothing to worry about from Dad or Mom."

"I have already, but you still need to honor Christine's feelings." He lifted a hand to Christine's chin, tipping it up until she was forced to meet his green eyes. This close she could see the gold flecks around the edges. She half expected to see anger or frustration for what she'd done, but he looked totally relaxed.

That made one of them.

"Christine makes the rules," he murmured and before she could react to that novel concept, he brushed his lips over hers.

The kiss started innocently enough. She had the mental wherewithal to register that his mouth was both soft and firm. He tasted of mint gum and whiskey, a combination that had her senses reeling.

She felt him begin to pull away and some small,

brave, underused part of her rebelled at the thought. She wound her arms around his neck and deepened the kiss, sensation skittering down her spine when their tongues mingled. A low moan erupted from her…or did the sound come from Gavin? The sound jolted her out of her lust-filled stupor and she jerked back. She'd had a couple glasses of wine, but not enough to excuse her basically mauling this man in front of his sister.

"I guess you guys are the real thing," Schuyler said with a laugh. "No one can fake that kind of chemistry."

"Right," Gavin murmured.

Christine kept her gaze on Schuyler. She had no idea what Gavin was thinking at the moment and was almost afraid to find out.

Schuyler wagged a finger at her brother. "Take care, big brother. Christine isn't like your usual girlfriends. She's special. Dad will kill you if you hurt her."

"I'm not going to hurt her," he said tightly, and Christine felt the arm still holding her go taut.

"He won't," she confirmed. She didn't need Schuyler reminding Gavin that she had nothing in common with the gorgeous, sexy women he usually dated. "He's amazing."

Schuyler laughed again. "If you say so. Shall we head back inside? I need a drink after this little bombshell."

"We'll meet you in there," Gavin said, and Christine wanted to argue. She wasn't quite ready to face his reaction to what she'd just done.

"Don't take too long," Schuyler told them, grinning at Christine. "Maddie should be throwing the bouquet soon. We need to position you front and center."

Christine tried to laugh, but it came out more like

a croak. "Sure," she managed and waved as Schuyler walked away.

When they were alone, she forced herself to turn to Gavin again. "I'm so—"

Her words were cut off as he fused his mouth to hers.

Gavin hadn't meant to kiss Christine again. He was still in shock from her announcement to Schuyler. He appreciated what she'd done. He'd been quickly running out of options when it came to distracting his sister from her obsession with his nonexistent girlfriend.

He owed her his thanks, but all he could think of was tasting her sweetness. His hands skimmed along the silky material of her dress, then over her hips, which held just the right amount of curve. And her reaction to him was a revelation. Straitlaced Christine Briscoe could kiss. She met him stroke for stroke, nipping at his bottom lip as if asking for more. Gavin lost himself in her, pulling her tight until her breasts pressed against his chest. As she had when they were dancing, she fit against him perfectly.

She was perfect.

How the hell had this happened?

Voices drifted from around the corner, and he took a step back, knowing the dazed look in her eyes probably mirrored the one in his.

"Hey, ladies," he called as a group of his mother's friends passed, several of them craning their necks to get a better look at Gavin and Christine.

He shifted so that he was shielding her from the curious gazes.

"We need to talk," he whispered when the women had passed.

Christine nodded, staring at the floor.

Gavin drew in a breath. Was she terrified of him now? She'd tried to save him from his sister, and he'd all but shoved his tongue down her throat. She'd seemed a willing participant at the time but now...

Another group of people turned the corner toward them, and Gavin automatically laced his fingers with Christine's and led her down the hall toward the hotel lobby. Her heels clicked against the pristine marble floors as they passed the stately columns that, along with the beautiful stained-glass dome, was the hallmark of the Driskill's famous lobby.

"Hey, Christine." The man she'd been standing with at the bar earlier, Bobby, waved from where he stood in front of the concierge desk. "A few of us are going to bail on the dancing and head to an Irish pub around the corner. Want to—"

"Oh, no," Christine whispered, her lips barely moving.

"She's busy," Gavin called and headed for the elevators along the far wall. She followed him in without protest but tugged her hand away as he hit the button for the fifth floor.

"Are you staying here, too?" he asked, not sure how to broach the subject of what had just happened between them. His wildly successful legal career had made Gavin believe he could talk his way out of any situation. Not so, apparently.

She shook her head, a lock of fiery hair falling forward to cover her cheek. Had he run his hands through her hair, loosening the elegant chignon? He couldn't remember but suddenly he wanted nothing more than to see the bright strands cascading over her shoulders.

He'd told his sister he was dating a woman with blue eyes and auburn hair. Maybe he'd been unconsciously thinking of Christine after their dance.

"Gavin, I—"

The door opened, cutting off whatever she was going to say to him. An older couple got in.

"Going down?" the man asked.

Gavin shook his head. "Up."

"We'll ride along," the woman offered. "You two look fancy."

"Wedding reception," Christine said quietly.

"I love weddings." The woman sighed. "Always so romantic."

Her husband snorted. "Except when your brother got sloshed and threw up on the dance floor at ours."

"He had food poisoning," the wife said, her tone clipped.

"Forty years." The man lifted his hands. "She still can't admit that her no-good brother's a drunk."

"At least he still shows up for holidays," the woman shot back. "Unlike your rude sister and her—"

"Our floor," Gavin interrupted when the elevator dinged. The door slid open, and he placed a hand on Christine's back. "I'm at the end of the hall," he told her when the door closed behind them with a snick.

His hand stilled as he realized her shoulders were shaking. Oh, God. Not tears. He could handle an angry jury or a recalcitrant witness. But tears killed him, especially the thought that he'd caused them.

"Don't cry," he whispered. "It will be—"

A sob broke from her throat. No, not a sob. Laughter.

She lifted her face, and he realized her tears weren't from anxiety, but amusement. "I know our relationship is five minutes long and a complete lie," she said, wiping her cheeks as she laughed, "but promise we'll never fight about your drunk brother."

He grinned and looped an arm around her shoulder as they started down the hall. "Fortunados can handle their liquor," he promised. "Do you have a sibling? I don't even know."

"A sister. Aimee is a year younger than me and perfect in every way."

"Perfection must run in the family."

As lines went, Gavin thought it was a pretty good one. Both subtle and charming. Christine only burst into another round of laughter. He was definitely losing his touch, although it was somewhat refreshing to be with a woman who didn't melt in a puddle at his feet. Gavin liked a challenge.

He wouldn't have pegged Christine as one, but this woman surprised him at every turn.

"I'm sorry," she whispered, clasping a hand over her mouth when a snort escaped.

He unlocked the hotel room door and gestured for her to enter.

"I hate to be indelicate," he said when they were both inside, "but are you drunk?"

She shook her head and drew in a shuddery breath. "It's just been a crazy night, you know?"

"I do. Would you like a drink now? I have a bottle of Mendoza red that was left in the welcome bag for wedding guests. Or water?"

"No, thanks." Now that her laughter had stopped, Gavin could almost see the wheels turning in Christine's brain as she became aware that she was alone with him in his hotel room.

"Would you feel more comfortable if I propped open the door?" He shrugged out of his jacket, tossing it onto the edge of the bed.

"I trust you," she whispered.

He blew out a breath, surprised at how happy the simple statement made him. He loosened his bow tie then undid the top button of his tailored shirt.

"Christine, I want to—"

"I'm sorry," she blurted. All the amusement from minutes ago had vanished from her features. "I shouldn't have butted into your conversation with Schuyler. You don't need my help to handle your sister and—"

"On the contrary. I want to thank you. You rescued me."

She wrapped her arms around her waist, and he could see her knuckles turning white from pressing her fingers against her rib cage. "I'm not sure what possessed me to get involved," she admitted. "I guess because you helped me with Bobby earlier."

"Bobby is a putz."

One side of her mouth curved, not a true smile but a step in the right direction. "That's true, which makes our situations different. Schuyler is your sister and she cares about you."

"She's also relentless." He took a step toward her, slowly, like he was approaching an animal that might spook at any moment. He didn't want to spook her. "Would you like to sit down?" He inclined his head toward the couch positioned in front of the room's large window. "We can talk about next steps."

Her cornflower-blue eyes widened. "Next steps. Okay."

He grabbed two bottles of water from the mini-fridge

and set them both on the coffee table before taking a seat next to her. "In case you get thirsty."

"You're really not mad?" She leaned forward and slipped off the heels she wore, revealing the most adorable painted pink toes Gavin had ever seen.

Hell, when was the last time he'd been with a woman? Granted, he'd been busy with work so his personal life had taken a back seat. But he was too far gone if a glimpse of toenail polish could mess with him like this.

"Christine, I'm grateful. I'd already made up a girlfriend. You made her a reality."

She tucked her legs underneath her. "And the kiss?"

"You'll never hear me complain about a beautiful woman kissing me."

She rolled her eyes. "I took it too far."

"You were convincing."

Color stained her cheeks. "Maybe I missed my calling. I should have been an actress."

"Hmm." Gavin didn't like the sound of that. It bothered him more than it should to think she'd been faking the kiss, even though that was what this whole thing was. A fake. He forced a smile, unwilling to let her see his reaction. Best to keep things light and casual, and he could do that better than almost anyone he knew. "I'm hoping you'll be interested in a repeat performance."

Christine made a sound that was somewhere between a yelp and whimper. "Of the kiss?"

Hell, yes.

"Actually, I was talking about you acting as my girlfriend." He ran a hand through his hair. "While I'm in Austin for the next few weeks."

"Weeks?" She uncurled her legs and dropped her feet to the thick carpet. For a moment he thought she was going to bolt. Then she placed her elbows on her legs and rested her head in her hands. "Weeks," she repeated on a slow exhalation.

"I'll make it worth your while."

Her head snapped up. "Like I'm a hooker?"

"Of course not." He shifted closer. "What I meant to say was it will be easy for you."

"You think I'm easy?"

"No. God, no." He leaned back, raised his gaze to the ceiling, hoping for some way to salvage this conversation. When he found no inspiration from above, he looked at Christine again, only to find her grinning at him. "That was a joke?"

She nodded. "You're different than I thought you'd be," she said quietly. "Not quite as perfect as you look at first glance."

"Is that a compliment or a criticism?"

She bit down on that full lower lip, and his insides clenched. "A compliment. It's good to know you're human."

"I don't usually like it when people tease me," he admitted.

"Oh."

"I like it with you."

"I'm glad." Another smile, this one almost shy. "I know you don't think I'm an easy hooker. You want me to pretend to be your girlfriend so your family leaves you alone. We'd have a fake relationship. That sounds simple."

Did it? Gavin wasn't sure what to make of his feelings for Christine, but they definitely weren't simple.

"Right," he agreed anyway. "One of the law firm's larger clients is based in Austin and we're finalizing a merger with another financial institution. Everything should be complete by the end of the month. It makes sense that we'd be together now, and then when I go back to Denver, you can break up with me."

"Like anyone is going to believe that," she said with a harsh laugh.

"Long distance relationships are tough. I don't think it will come as a huge surprise."

"The part where *I* break up with *you* is going to be the surprise." She sat back on the sofa, so close that he could feel the warmth of her body. "Your family knows you're a bit of a playboy."

"Am not."

She rolled her eyes. "How many women have you dated?"

He thought about that, grimaced. "Since when?"

"I rest my case," she told him.

"But this is different." He took her hand, laced their fingers together and looked directly into her eyes. "You've changed me."

Chapter Three

Christine felt her mouth go dry at his words. She'd changed him?

"At least that's what my family needs to believe," he clarified.

"Schuyler agreed not to tell anyone," Christine argued, although the thought of how she'd go about convincing people that she and Gavin were really a thing made goose bumps dance along her skin. Talk about the adventure of a lifetime.

"We *told* her not to tell anyone." He traced his thumb in circles against the sensitive skin on the inside of her wrist. "But there's no way she's going to be able to resist."

"So we'll need to convince your family this is real," she whispered. "Your parents will be upset they didn't know."

"They'll understand," he assured her. "I'll make sure they do."

"I hate lying to your father…to anyone in your family. They've been so good to me."

"This isn't going to change anything," he promised.

But Christine knew nothing would ever be the same. She should stop this charade right now, march downstairs and explain to Schuyler that it was all a big misunderstanding. Although she was sober, maybe she could pretend to be drunk. Blaming her crazy behavior on alcohol might give her a decent excuse.

Gavin's jacket began to ring. He stood and moved toward the bed, pulling his phone out of the pocket of the discarded tuxedo coat.

"Hey, sis," he said into the device. "No, I'm not coming back down." Pause. "Yes, she's with me." Pause. "I don't think she's going to care about the bouquet." Pause with an added eye roll. "Don't go there, Schuyler. I told you this is special. She's special. Let me enjoy it, okay?" Pause. "I understand and appreciate it. I love you, too." Pause. "Okay, I'll see you at the brunch in the morning."

He punched the screen to end the call then tossed the phone on the bed again.

"You missed the bouquet."

Christine stood. "I'm okay with that. You shouldn't be annoyed with Schuyler for calling. I don't want this to complicate things with you and your family."

He moved toward her. "My family is always complicated, especially now that the Fortunes are involved. My only concern is you. As much as I appreciate what you did earlier, if you aren't okay with this arrangement, we'll end it."

Here was her chance. A dance, a few kisses and she'd

go back to her normal life before the clock struck midnight, like some sort of Fortune-inspired Cinderella.

But she couldn't force her mouth to form the words. Despite this whole thing being fake, she wasn't going to miss her chance at getting to know Gavin. Under what other circumstances would a man like him choose to date someone like her?

Not that she was down on herself. Christine liked her life and felt comfortable with who she was. Usually. But she wasn't the type of woman who could catch Gavin Fortunado's attention. Until now.

"I don't want it to end," she said, embarrassed that she sounded breathless.

Gavin didn't seem to notice. He cupped her cheeks in his hands. "Me neither," he whispered and kissed her. Once again it felt like fireworks exploding through her body. The kiss was sweet and passionate at the same time. He seemed in no hurry to speed things along, content to take his time as he explored her lips.

Then his mouth trailed over her jaw and along her throat, her skin igniting from the touch. He tugged on the strap of her dress, and it fell down her shoulder. He kissed his way from the base of her neck to her collarbone. Her body was all heat and need. She wanted so much from this moment that she couldn't even put it all into words.

"You're so beautiful," he whispered.

The compliment was like a bucket of ice water dumped over her head. She wrenched away, yanking her dress strap back into place.

"Don't say that," she told him, shaking her head. "You don't have to say that."

Confusion clouded his vivid green eyes. "In my experience, women like to hear those words."

She swallowed. How was she supposed to respond without sounding like she was fishing for something more? That wasn't the case at all. In fact, she felt the opposite. She didn't want or need him to tell her she was beautiful because it simply wasn't true.

Christine prided herself on being pragmatic about her appearance. Growing up, she'd been a chubby girl with thick glasses and bright red hair that was more frizz than curls. Her mom had forced her to keep it in frizzy Annie-style curls that were anything but flattering. Christine had spent years enduring teasing, much of it led by her younger sister, until she'd become an expert at not being seen.

Aimee, with her larger-than-life personality and classic beauty, had been happy to step into the spotlight. She went to parties and on dates, while Christine spent most of her high school years in her room reading or listening to music. No one in her family seemed to notice or care as she slipped further into the periphery of their lives.

She'd decided to change things when she went away to college. She'd gotten contacts and started running, shedding the excess pounds that had plagued her for years. A bevy of expensive hair products helped her tame her wild mane, and the color had mellowed from the bright orange of her childhood. Her dad had called her "baby carrot" as a kid, and her sister had amended the nickname to "jumbo carrot" due to Christine's size. Even though she thankfully hadn't heard the nickname in years, it was how she still thought of herself.

She took pains with her appearance and she knew

she wasn't ugly. She was decent-looking, in fact. But beautiful? No, not to someone like Gavin.

"This is not real," she said, both for his sake and to remind herself.

Gavin's thick brows furrowed. "That doesn't mean—"

"What's your favorite color?"

"Um...blue."

"Mine's purple." She crossed her arms over her chest, aware he was still staring at her like he couldn't quite follow the direction of her thoughts. Join the club. Her mind and heart felt like they'd survived an emotional tornado, hurricane and maybe a tsunami thrown in for good measure, all in one night. "Favorite food?"

"Pizza."

"I like burgers and fries."

His mouth quirked. "That's kind of cute."

"Burgers aren't cute."

"You're admitting you like them as opposed to giving me some line about loving salmon and kale. That's cute."

"I take yoga classes and run before work. What do you do to work out?"

One brow arched. "So you're flexible?"

With a groan, she stepped around him toward the hotel room desk. "Do you want me to write all this down?" She picked up a pen and the small pad of paper with the hotel's logo.

"The ways you're flexible?"

"Gavin, be serious. You were the one who said your family would find out about us. We need to have our stories straight." Christine clutched the pen and paper to her chest and fought the urge to whimper as Gavin ran a hand through his hair. She could see the muscles of his arm flexing under his white shirt. "When did we meet?"

"We've known each other for years."

"Right. I mean when did we—"

"It was Thanksgiving break my senior year of college. I was getting ready to retake the LSAT after my not-so-stellar performance the first time around."

Christine inclined her head, surprised and charmed he'd remember the very first time they met. "You were studying in the conference room at the Fortunado Real Estate office. It was quiet because of the holiday."

"And I was bitter because my buddies had flown to Aspen for the weekend." He started undoing the buttons of his shirt, casually, as if it wasn't a big deal for him to be undressing in front of her. Of course, he wore a white T-shirt under the formal shirt, so it wasn't a true striptease.

Christine's heart stammered just the same.

"You were the only one in the office," he continued. "You kept bringing me coffee and takeout."

She shrugged. "It was my first week working for your father and I wanted to be helpful in any way I could."

"Do you remember what you told me after I'd complained to you for the millionth time about life being unfair?"

She shook her head. She hadn't remembered speaking to him at all. She'd graduated college a semester early and had felt lucky to be hired by Kenneth right away. It had taken almost a year on the job before she believed her boss wouldn't walk into the office and tell her he'd made a horrible mistake taking a chance on her. Having Gavin in the office during the quiet lull of the Thanksgiving holiday had made her so nervous. All she'd been able to do was refill his mug and send out for sandwiches.

"You told me to channel my inner Elle Woods."

Christine gave a soft chuckle. "I loved *Legally Blonde*."

"Clearly. You gushed about the movie. I didn't know what you were talking about," Gavin said with a grin. "I went back to my parents' house and rented it."

"You watched *Legally Blonde*?"

"Oh, yeah. I not only watched it, I was also inspired. I mean, if Elle Woods could get into law school, what excuse did I have?"

She snorted a laugh then pressed her hand to her mouth. "Tell me you didn't use scented pink paper for your admissions application."

"Not exactly." Gavin draped the crisp white shirt over the back of the desk chair then held up his hands, palms out. "If you tell anyone I said I was inspired by that movie, I'll deny it. But I might have Reese Witherspoon to thank for my law career." His smile softened. "And you."

Christine felt her mouth drop open. "I...had no idea."

"It seemed like a stupid thing to admit at the time. But I've never forgotten. You helped me then, and now you're saving my bacon once again. I owe you, Christine."

"It's not a big deal," she said automatically. But it was. It was that time he'd spent in the office poring over law books that had given her an initial glimpse of who Gavin truly was on the inside. Through the years she'd remained convinced he was more than the rakish attorney who was always scaling mountains or hurling himself down ski slopes in his off time. Back then he'd been nervous, vulnerable, and she hadn't been able to resist him. Just like she couldn't now.

She lifted the paper and pen. "We should still go over some more details if we're going to make this relationship believable." Not that it would be difficult on her part. One look at her face and it would be clear to everyone that she was already half in love with Gavin.

"How about we watch a movie while we talk?" He winked. "Elle Woods for old times' sake?"

"Sure," she whispered.

He picked up his jacket then patted the bed. "Make yourself comfortable. I'm going to order something from late-night room service. Can I tempt you with a hamburger?"

Christine started to shake her head but her stomach rumbled. "No cheese and medium-well, please."

He nodded. "Got it."

She placed the paper and pen on the nightstand and climbed onto the bed, butterflies racing across her stomach. She was in Gavin's bed. Or *on* it. Close enough.

He used the room's landline to place the order then clicked the remote to turn on the TV, searching until he found *Legally Blonde*. "I haven't watched this movie in years," he told her.

"It holds up," she said, choosing not to share that the movie was on her regular rotation of Saturday night rom-coms. It struck her that tonight was Saturday and here she sat watching a movie, as had become her weekly routine. Only tonight instead of curling up with her black lab, Diana, she was in one of the most beautiful hotels in Austin with Gavin.

She loved her dog, but this was way better.

Her nerves disappeared as soon as the movie started. She and Gavin talked and laughed, and then ate when the food arrived. He cleared the empty plates when the movie ended, placing the tray outside the hotel room door.

"I think you should stay a bit longer," he said, checking his watch. "The reception isn't scheduled to end until midnight, and knowing my family, they'll be closing down the place."

"I don't want to keep you from going to sleep," she said, stifling a yawn.

"Apparently, I'm not the one who's tired."

"It's been a kind of crazy night for me," she admitted.

"If you want to go I can—"

"We could watch another movie?" She smiled. "Something with lots of action to keep us awake."

"Good idea." He returned to the bed and flipped through channels until he found an old James Bond flick.

"Who's your favorite Bond?" she asked.

"Sean Connery." He moved to the center of the mattress. "In case you're interested, I make a pretty good pillow."

Her girl parts went wild. She scooted closer, and he lifted one arm, tucking her against his chest.

"I bet you're a Daniel Craig fan," he said, resting his chin on the top of her head.

"Every woman with a pulse is a fan of Daniel Craig."

She felt his chuckle against her ear, and the rhythmic up and down of his chest. As bizarre as the night had been, it was the stuff of her fantasies to be cuddling with Gavin. If only the night never had to end.

Chapter Four

Christine blinked awake, disoriented for a moment at the unfamiliar surroundings. The something—someone—moved next to her and the previous night came flooding back.

She turned to find Gavin asleep next to her, lying chest down with his hair rumpled and a shadow of stubble covering his jaw. Somehow they'd both ended up under the covers. He still wore his white T-shirt, and she was in her dress. The last thing she remembered was James Bond being served a shaken-not-stirred martini.

Now pale light spilled in from the room's picture window. She glanced at the clock on the nightstand. Seven in the morning.

Well, she'd successfully missed the end of the reception, but if she didn't leave quickly, she might run into the Fortunado family heading to breakfast.

With as little movement as possible, she slipped out of the bed. Gavin made a snuffling sound but didn't wake. Christine grabbed her shoes and purse. Without bothering to look in the mirror, she let herself out of the room.

She didn't need to see her reflection to know that she wasn't a pretty sight. She had no intention of allowing Gavin to see her this way, either.

The door closed with a soft snick, and she turned, only to come face-to-face with Valene, the baby of the Fortunado clan.

Her brown eyes widened. "Hey, Christine."

Christine smoothed a hand over her tumbling hair. "Hi, Val. Going to work out?"

Valene wore athletic shorts and a fitted tank top. Earbuds dangled from either side of her head. Her wavy blond hair was pulled back in a high ponytail. "Yeah. How about you?" One delicate brow rose. "That's Gavin's room, right?"

"Is it?" Christine's voice was a croak.

"And you're wearing the same dress from the wedding last night," Valene pointed out, none too helpfully as far as Christine was concerned. "Schuyler said Gavin left the reception early because he wasn't feeling well."

"I think he's okay now," Christine answered, purposely ignoring the question in the other woman's dark eyes. "Well, I should be going. Have a great day."

Without waiting for a response, she hurried down the hall, only taking a few steps before realizing that she'd be waiting for the elevator with Valene. Why did decisions made late at night rarely hold up to the light of day?

She breathed a sigh of relief when she noticed the

sign for the stairs, pushing open the door and racing down four flights. The stairwell led out to the parking garage. She shoved her feet back into the heels and made it to her Subaru hatchback and then away from the hotel without seeing anyone else she knew.

Thank heaven for small favors.

Quite small since she understood that although Valene had been shocked enough to allow Christine to escape this morning, there would be no avoiding the Fortunado sisters for long. Valene worked out of the real estate agency's Houston office but visited Austin regularly to help with establishing a new client base. Even if she didn't see Valene right away, the sisters would talk. Gavin seemed sure they didn't have anything to worry about, but Christine remained unconvinced.

Walking into her condo, she was greeted with an enthusiastic bark. Diana trotted toward her, tail wagging and ears pricked up. Christine smiled despite her tumbling emotions. Nothing like unconditional love to work as a distraction.

"Hey, girl." Christine crouched down to love on the dog. "Did Jackson take good care of you last night?" At ten years old, Diana was fairly mellow and low maintenance. As she did on nights when she worked late, Christine had asked her neighbor's preteen son to dogsit Diana.

The dog pressed her head against Christine and gave a soft snort, making the tension in her shoulders lessen slightly. "Let me shower and change, and we'll go for a walk."

The dog turned in a happy circle at the mention of her favorite word.

"You would not believe the night I had," Christine

said as she placed her purse on the counter and headed for the bathroom, Diana following close on her heels. The dog had been her roommate and companion for so long, she thought nothing of carrying on a one-sided conversation.

She told Diana about Gavin and their arrangement. The dog inclined her head, as if truly listening. Christine was grateful for the sympathetic canine ear. Most of her girlfriends were in the real estate industry or knew the Fortunados, so she couldn't share the arrangement with any of them.

Her sister would have a field day giving Christine grief about only being able to find a fake boyfriend. Even as adults, their relationship was fraught with teasing, all one-sided. Christine had never allowed herself to think much of it, although it was strange that they couldn't seem to shake their childhood roles.

Aimee was beautiful, popular and funny. She worked as a hairdresser in a busy salon in one of Austin's tonier suburbs. She had tons of friends, a steady stream of rich boyfriends and remained the apple of their father's eye. Yet she never seemed to tire of pointing out Christine's shortcomings.

It had been easier when Christine lived in Houston. She'd come up with plenty of excuses over the years as to why she could only return to Austin once or twice a year for family functions.

But now that she'd moved back to her hometown, her mother made it clear she expected to see more of her.

After her shower, she dressed in a sweatshirt and loose jeans, laced up her sneakers and headed out the door with Diana. As always, the dog was thrilled to check out the scents along the walking trail situated about a block from the condo.

Christine waved to neighbors and tried to keep her thoughts from straying to Gavin. Why had she agreed to be his pretend girlfriend?

She had no answer, other than the fact that it was her best—and possibly only—chance of ever spending time with him.

Maybe that was a good enough reason.

Diana whined softly as they got to the open meadow that bordered the trail. Christine unclipped the dog's leash, and Diana sped off to investigate the nearby trees.

Christine's phone dinged, and she pulled it out of her pocket, drawing in a quick breath at the text message.

I missed you this morning. Talk soon?

She and Gavin had exchanged numbers in his hotel room, but it still shocked her to see his name on the screen.

How to respond?

Last night had been one of the best of her life, even though nothing had happened between them. Okay, she was disappointed nothing had happened. She'd spent the night in a man's bed and all he'd done was snuggle her. Did that say more about Gavin or her? She was afraid the answer was the latter.

Yes, she knew he respected her and she'd heard him tell his sister that Christine was special. Now, that felt like an excuse for keeping things basically platonic between them.

But he missed her.

That was a good sign, right?

She tapped in the start of several responses and almost immediately deleted each of them. Too sweet. Too trite. Trying too hard.

Finally, she sent a smiley-face emoji.

And immediately regretted it. Her mother sent smiley-face emojis about everything. All Christine needed was to add an "LOL" along with several exclamation points and she'd officially become the fuddy-duddy she was afraid might be her destiny.

Diana barked at a squirrel, and Christine pocketed the phone with a sigh. She wasn't sure what she'd gotten herself into with Gavin Fortunado, but there was no doubt she was in over her head.

"Where's Christine?"

Gavin made a show of checking his watch as Schuyler dropped into the chair next to him. For the morning-after brunch she'd traded her bridesmaid dress for a pair of slim trousers and a pale pink sweater, her blond hair in a low ponytail. He had the sudden urge to tug on it, as he had to annoy her when they were kids. "It's ten o'clock. Isn't that too early for an interrogation?"

"One question does not an interrogation make," she countered, forking up a piece of pineapple and popping it into her mouth.

"Hey, you two." His youngest sister, Valene, slipped into the chair on his other side. She wore a gray sheath dress and an understated pendant necklace around her neck. When had the baby of the family grown up so much? "What's the deal with you and Christine?" she asked Gavin.

He glared at Schuyler. "So much for keeping things on the down low."

"I didn't say anything," she told him, arching a brow at Valene.

"She didn't need to." Val sipped her glass of orange juice. "I caught Christine doing the walk of shame from your room this morning on my way to work out."

"Seriously?" Schuyler demanded, eyes narrowing. But to Gavin's utter shock, her stare was focused on Valene and not him. "You worked out already? Stop making me feel like a slacker, Val."

Val rolled her eyes and winked at Gavin. "So…"

"She wasn't doing the walk of shame," Gavin said through clenched teeth, wishing for something stronger than coffee in his china cup.

"Don't get me wrong," Valene told him, ignoring Schuyler's continued glare. "I approve. She's a definite improvement over that bimbo you were dating when I came to Denver last year."

"She's probably too good for you," Schuyler added absently. "How did you get her to take you on in the first place?"

"Feels like an interrogation," Gavin muttered under his breath.

Schuyler chuckled. "You know I'm joking. You're a catch, Gavin."

"It's just a surprise that you've let yourself be caught." Valene bit into a slice of bagel slathered with cream cheese.

"I don't want to talk about this with either of you." He inclined his head toward the rest of the family, who were gathered around Maddie and Zach on the other side of the room. "Especially not here."

"You need our expertise," Schuyler told him. "Christine is amazing. She's the kind of woman…"

"I'd want at my side for always," Gavin whispered, unaware that he'd spoken aloud until both of his sisters gasped.

Schuyler grabbed his arm. "Are you saying…"

"Did you ask her to marry you?" Valene leaned closer. "Are you and Christine engaged?"

Gavin felt his Adam's apple bob in his throat as he swallowed hard. "I didn't say that."

"It's true, though. I can tell by the look in your eyes." Valene let out a little squeal of delight then lifted her bagel and smiled blandly at the group sitting at the next table. "Try the blueberry cream cheese. It's amazing."

"Can you two be more obvious?" Gavin tugged his arm out of Schuyler's grasp.

"You're getting *married*," Schuyler told him, and he didn't dare contradict her. "You can't keep it a secret."

Fake dating to fake engaged in twenty-four hours. His stomach pitched as he thought about Christine's reaction to this new development.

"And there's no reason to." Valene dabbed at the corner of her mouth with a napkin. "Everyone loves Christine."

"She's a private person," he said, realizing the excuse sounded lame.

Schuyler nodded just the same. "I get that, but she's like one of the family to us. She's going to be one of the family soon. How soon? Have you set a date?"

He shook his head, trying to reel in his thoughts. What was he doing here? "Not yet. We didn't want to take any attention from Maddie and Zach."

Both of his sisters nodded in agreement.

"I'm sure that was Christine's idea," Valene said. "She's so thoughtful. We'll make sure she knows how welcome she is." She looked past him, her eyes widening. "Oh, they brought out a fresh tray of pastries. I need to get to them before Everett and Connor snag the best ones." She pushed back from the table. "I'll be right back. Who wants a donut?"

"Me." Schuyler raised her hand. "Bring one for Gavin, too. He's probably hangry and hungover."

"I'm neither," he said, although his head was starting to ache. Was it too early for a shot? "But I'll take a Bloody Mary, please."

Valene laughed as she walked away.

Schuyler wasted no time. She turned to Gavin and started in on him again. "Christine is going to get the wrong impression if you try to keep her a secret much longer, especially since you're in Austin for the rest of the month. She needs to start wedding planning, and I can help. Think about it, Gavin. She's going to be your wife. I get the business about being private, but if you make her feel like everything's okay, she'll believe it."

"Do you think I haven't?"

"I think you don't have much experience with a woman who you can be proud to bring home to Mom and Dad."

"That's not—" Gavin stopped, ran a hand through his hair. It was exactly the truth. Even though his relationship with Christine was a complete fake, he hadn't dated anyone with her amount of class and elegance in years. Christine was the kind of woman a man thought of spending his life with, and Gavin's stomach pitched at the realization.

"Bring her to the family reunion," Schuyler told him, breaking into his tumbling thoughts.

"What family reunion?"

"The one I'm planning to introduce everyone to the new Fortunes."

He shook his head. "I thought *we* were the new Fortunes."

She leaned forward, her eyes dancing with excitement. "There are more, Gavin. Dad has a half brother, Miles. He lives in New Orleans and has seven kids. Ben and Keaton put me in touch with the youngest son, Nolan. He's recently moved to Austin."

Ben Fortune Robinson had spearheaded the search for his illegitimate siblings after discovering that his tech mogul father was really Jerome Fortune, who'd faked his death years earlier. Jerome reinvented himself as Gerald Robinson and built his tech empire, but in recent years the family's focus had been on their new siblings. Keaton Whitfield, a British architect who was now living in Austin, had been the first of the secret illegitimate Fortunes Ben had tracked down. Together, the two of them had worked to uncover Gerald's other grown children and bring them into the fold.

Schuyler was the Fortune expert as far as Gavin was concerned, so he knew from her that Gerald's estranged wife, Charlotte, had actually known about his other children for the duration of their marriage and hidden the information from everyone. To learn there were even more previously unknown Fortunes out there… Gavin didn't know what to think.

"Schuyler, last year you were the one who wasn't sure if the Fortunes could be trusted. That was the whole basis for you infiltrating the family through the Mendozas."

She smiled wistfully. "Thank heavens for that brilliant idea. Otherwise, I never would have met Carlo."

"Can we keep on topic?" Gavin asked. Once again he wondered what it would have felt like to grow up an only child.

"We have to welcome the New Orleans Fortunes into the family, just like the Robinsons did for us. They're as innocent in all the family intrigue as we were, but we can't deny the connection. I'm going to make sure it goes well." She rubbed her hands together. "The reunion is going to be held at the Mendoza Winery. Nolan seems like a good guy. He promised he'd get his brothers and sisters to attend. I'm not sure about his parents yet, but I'm still hopeful."

"You never give up," Gavin murmured with a smile.

"It's one of my best traits," she answered. "I think the Fortune Robinson siblings are going to come, as well. I talked to Ben last week and he seemed amenable to the idea."

"What does Dad think of all this?"

Schuyler shrugged. "He's going back to enjoying his retirement after Maddie and Zach return from their mini-honeymoon, but I know he's curious about our new extended family. He and Mom have agreed to drive up and meet everyone. We'll all be here. Except maybe Connor. I'm not sure about his schedule and you know how dedicated he is to the search firm. He promised to try. Either way, the rest of the Fortunados will show a united front in welcome."

"It looks like you've worked out all the details."

"I'm doing my best. Now that Maddie's happily married, I can turn even more of my attention to the reunion." She wiggled her eyebrows. "And to making sure you don't mess things up with Christine before your big day."

I can't mess up something that doesn't really exist, Gavin thought to himself. Although he wasn't sure that rationale actually held water. It felt as if he'd already made a huge misstep by asking her to enter into a fake relationship.

He actually liked Christine quite a bit. More than he'd expected and definitely more than he had any other woman he'd recently dated. But it would complicate things if he tried to turn their pretend love into something real. Plus, despite what his sisters now believed, he still barely knew her. There was no explaining the connection he felt between them, yet he couldn't deny it.

"Don't tell me you've already done something stupid," Schuyler said, studying his face.

"No," he answered automatically then schooled his features. His sister was far too perceptive for his own good.

"You'll bring her to the reunion?" she asked again.

"You know she wants to keep our relationship private," Gavin argued weakly. "A Fortune reunion is the least private activity I can imagine."

Schuyler waved away his concern. "Valene saw her leaving your room, so someone else might have, as well. Besides, she'll want to start planning the wedding. Does she have a dress yet?"

"Um...I don't think so."

"Val and I will take her shopping. We have to plan the perfect bridal shower, too."

"Slow down, Schuyler." Gavin held up a hand like he was giving a command to an eager puppy. "All of this is going to overwhelm her. I don't want that. Even though we're engaged, Christine and I are going to take things at our own pace. If she wants—"

"You're in Austin until the end of the month, right?" his sister interrupted.

"Yes."

"Then it's no longer a long-distance romance where you can sweep her off to Colorado and have her all to yourself." She speared a piece of melon from her plate. "I assume that's what you've been doing. Unless you've been secretly coming to Austin for clandestine dates? Where did you get engaged, anyway?"

Gavin's heart started to leap in his chest. There were so many moving parts in this situation. He needed to talk to Christine to make sure they both kept them all straight. Hell, he wanted to talk to Christine again just to hear her voice.

"Colorado," he told his sister, deciding it was best to stay away from any pesky details. "Everything has been in Colorado."

"That makes sense," she agreed.

Good thing it did to someone.

"Austin is different than a lot of places. It's a big small town in some ways. You know that. It would be silly for you to try to keep things a secret, and I doubt it would work anyway. If you talk to Mom and Dad, they'll understand, but you can't keep trying to hide it. Mom will drive you crazy with attempts to nose into your love life, anyway."

Gavin pointed his fork at Schuyler. "I guess you get it honestly."

"Does that mean you'll bring Christine to the reunion?"

Out of the corner of his eye, Gavin saw Everett and Lila approaching the table. He might have to take his sister's advice and go public with his relationship with

Christine, but he didn't intend to reveal it this morning. "I'll invite her," he promised, "but the decision whether to attend will be hers."

"Oh, we can convince her," Schuyler assured him with a smile.

"No pressure," he said, pushing back from the table. "I mean it. I don't want you or Maddie or Valene to make her feel like she has to accept."

"Gavin, you have a protective side when it comes to your future bride." Schuyler grinned. "It's adorable."

He shook his head. "I'm going to talk to Mom and Dad. Let me tell them about Christine and the engagement, okay?"

"Sure," Schuyler agreed. "But I've already told you, the family loves her as much as you obviously do. There's nothing to worry about."

Gavin's stomach pitched at the mention of the *L* word. Those four letters were definitely cause for concern. Fearing that Schuyler would be able to read his emotions, he turned to greet Everett and Lila then made his way toward the rest of the family at the other side of the room.

He knew he needed to talk to his parents about Christine but didn't relish the thought of lying to them outright about his relationship. He told himself it would be better if he waited to speak to his dad in private. Although guilt sat heavy in his gut, he made it through the rest of the brunch then retreated back to his room, changed into a T-shirt and sweatpants and headed out for a run.

He expected to miss the bright sunshine and crisp air in Colorado but it felt good to be back in Texas. After a four-mile loop around downtown Austin, he showered, changed and then texted Christine to see if she could have dinner.

The challenge was knowing what to call the invitation. A fake date? A business meeting? In the end, he left it at "Want to grab dinner?"

His chest constricted when her return text lit up his screen. She had plans for the evening. Should he read more into the terse message? Was she angry that he'd texted instead of phoning? Could she be regretting their agreement enough to call off their arrangement?

Disappointment crashed through him, both because she wasn't available and due to the thought of her possibly backing out of the pretend relationship.

This discontent was new for him. Gavin didn't usually allow himself much time for reflection or self-analysis. Deep thoughts weren't really his deal. As a middle child in a big family, he'd learned early on that the best way to get noticed was action as opposed to introspection, which suited his restless nature just fine.

He'd climbed trees, raced his bike along dirt paths and generally careened through his childhood with an abandon that seemed to both amuse and terrify his parents. He knew they'd been happy when he finally settled on law school, and the constant challenges in his professional life kept his adrenaline moving just like the extreme sports he loved. But lately mastering even the most technical ski slopes hadn't been taxing enough to help him feel settled at the end of the day. Not like he had spending the night with Christine curled next to him.

He had friends in Austin who would be up for a night out, but the idea of going out with anyone but his fake girlfriend held no appeal. In the end, he pulled out his laptop and got to work preparing for the meeting he had scheduled with the firm's client next week.

His fingers itched to call Christine, but she hadn't given him any indication in her text that she wanted to talk to him. Not even a smiley-face emoji like the one she'd sent earlier. The simple plan for getting his family to stay out of his love life was already far more complicated than he'd expected.

Chapter Five

When the knock sounded on her office door Monday morning, Christine was already on pins and needles. She hadn't talked to Gavin other than a simple text about dinner the previous night. When she'd texted back that she had plans, he hadn't responded and she'd been too nervous to suggest an alternate time to get together.

She imagined him having second, third and fourth thoughts about their arrangement, especially after spending what to him must have been a boring night in his hotel room. Falling asleep after watching movies together—talk about a wasted moment. She figured she'd never get the chance for a do-over.

Maddie and Zach had flown to Cabo for a short mini-honeymoon. Neither of them was willing to leave the Austin branch for too long when business was picking up so much. Christine had no doubt they trusted her

to run the internal side of things at the office, and Valene had postponed her return to Houston until they got
back. Even Kenneth was pitching in despite his recent
retirement. But she still appreciated their commitment
and understood their mutual dedication to Fortunado
Real Estate was part of what made them such a perfect couple.

Christine might have had a crush on Gavin for years,
but what did they really have in common? She loved her
work and knew he enjoyed his law career, but that was
where the similarities ended. He was a high-powered
corporate attorney who worked with big-name clients,
and she was more comfortable behind the scenes, keeping everyone in the office organized and on track. She
led a quiet life, and he was always off on some new adventure during his downtime.

It had pained her to say no to his dinner invitation
last night, even if she was sure he was offering because
they needed to confirm their stories before revealing
their relationship to his family. But since she'd moved
back to Austin, her mother had insisted she come to dinner every Sunday, sitting down to a meal with her parents and sister. And if she needed a physical reminder
of why she and Gavin weren't a great match, her sister,
Aimee, was more than happy to provide it.

Aimee was a talented hairstylist but had trouble holding down a job, bouncing from salon to salon so often
that only her most loyal clients stayed with her. Still,
she always made wherever she landed sound like the
most exciting place on the planet to work. Her sister rel-
ished every opportunity to point out what a boring life
Christine led and how old-fashioned it was to stick with
the same company for a decade. Last night had been

no exception. The owner of Aimee's most recent salon had invited her to go to the Bahamas for a weekend. Although the guy sounded like a total creep to Christine, her sister insisted Christine was just too much of a stick-in-the-mud to appreciate an opportunity for adventure.

Someone knocked again, more insistently this time, and Christine realized she'd been lost in her own thoughts.

"Come in," she called, pasting the polite smile on her face she knew any of her coworkers would expect to see.

Her jaw dropped when Gavin walked into her small office, and it felt like all the air in the room had been sucked out the moment he entered.

She shut her mouth and attempted to draw a breath but ended up choking and sputtering, reaching for the glass of water next to her computer. Her hand tipped it and water spilled across her desk.

With a yelp-cough, she jumped up, at least having enough sense to pluck the stack of contracts she'd been inputting before they were soaked through. She rushed to the utility closet in the corner of the office and grabbed a roll of paper towels, turning back to find Gavin lifting her wireless keyboard and phone out of the water.

"What a mess," she muttered then quickly cleaned up the spilled water, still coughing every few seconds.

She could feel her face flaming with embarrassment. Only when she'd dumped the last of the wet paper towels in the trash can next to her desk did she look up at Gavin.

"You're cute when you're flustered," he said, tossing the paper towels he'd used to dry the bottom of the keyboard and her cell phone case into the trash.

She gave a small laugh, which turned into a cough.

"Going to make it?" he asked, arching one thick brow.

"I'm fine," she whispered and took the phone and keyboard from him. "Mortified, but fine. Coordination isn't always my thing."

He winked, and her stomach felt like it had taken the first plunge on a roller-coaster ride. "Good to know."

"I didn't expect to see you here." She busied herself with rearranging the items on her desk, trying to ignore how close Gavin stood and how her body reacted to him.

"I'm meeting with my dad in—" he checked his watch "—five minutes."

"Oh." Disappointment washed through her at the knowledge that he hadn't stopped by to see her. Of course, why would he stop by for her when he could easily—

"Are you free for lunch after?"

Her mouth dropped open again and she pressed it shut. "Mmmhrmrh."

One side of his mouth quirked. "Is that a yes?"

"Yes," she breathed and was rewarded with a full grin.

It was like being struck with a two-by-four. She felt dazed, like she'd held her breath too long and was getting light-headed from the sensation.

Okay, maybe she was light-headed. *Breathe. Remember to breathe.*

"I'd like to speak to my dad about us," Gavin continued like she wasn't having an internal freak-out inches away from him. "If that's okay with you?"

"Us?" she squeaked.

"Our relationship."

"Our *fake* relationship," she clarified.

"Yes, well…" He massaged a hand along the back of his neck, and she wondered if she wasn't the only one trying to hide her nerves. "What would you think about a pretend engagement?"

Christine choked out shocked laugh. "Excuse me?"

"I…uh…my sisters… There was a little…uh…misunderstanding at breakfast the morning after the wedding."

"A misunderstanding that ended up with us engaged?" she asked, pressing her palms to her cheeks, which felt like they were on fire.

"It's not much different than dating."

The sound that came from her throat sounded like the creaking of the old screen door at her parents' house.

"I'm sorry, Christine." He started to reach for her then rubbed his neck again. "I should have said something, but they were so happy about it. I thought an engagement might be…uh…fun."

"Fun," she repeated. She started to shake her head, but Gavin was looking at her with so much hope that she couldn't stand to disappoint him. It was what she told herself but only part of the truth. She also didn't want her time with Gavin—pretend or not—to end. "Sure. It could be fun."

"Really?"

She smiled when Gavin's voice cracked on the word like a teenage boy.

"Yes," she confirmed and when he grinned, she had to believe she'd made the right decision. "So you're going to tell your dad we're engaged?"

He nodded. "Before I speak with him, I wanted to

make sure you hadn't changed your mind about the arrangement and now the engagement. When you blew me off last night, I wondered if—"

"I have Sunday dinner at my parents' every week," she interrupted. "The only thing that could get me out of it is a trip to the emergency room, and there's a good chance my mom would pack up the food and bring it to the hospital. She has this notion that eating a meal together will suddenly make the four of us into a happy family after almost three decades."

"That's great," Gavin murmured then shook his head at her frown. "I'm sorry. I don't mean it's great for you. It's not great that you have to deal with that, but I thought you were blowing me off."

She inclined her head as soft pink tinged his cheeks. Was Gavin Fortunado blushing?

"I wouldn't blow you off," she whispered, her voice sounding husky to her own ears. "Ever."

He drew in a breath like her words meant something to him. As if she meant something to him, which was impossible because before Saturday night they hadn't done much more than speak in passing throughout the past ten years.

Except he remembered the first time they'd met. He'd told her she'd helped convince him he could make it to law school.

Something tiny and tentative unfurled in Christine's heart. It felt a lot like hope. Possibility. Her chance for something more.

The same unfamiliar streak of boldness that had prompted her to act at the reception flashed through her again. She stepped forward, placed her hands on his broad shoulders, rose up on her tiptoes and then kissed him.

Their mouths melded together for a few seconds. She wouldn't allow it to go any further, not in her office. Even though the door was closed, several of her coworkers would feel no hesitation about knocking and walking right in.

When she started to pull away, Gavin gripped her hips with his big hands and squeezed. The touch reverberated through her body, sending shock waves of desire pulsing through her.

She moaned and then felt him smile against her lips. "I can't wait for lunch," he said, the rough timbre of his voice tickling her senses. "Suddenly, I'm starving."

Then he let her go, and she had to place a hand on the corner of her desk to steady herself.

Good gravy, the man could kiss.

"I'll meet you at the reception desk in twenty minutes?" he asked over his shoulder.

"Sure." She held up a hand to wave then pulled it to her side. What kind of a ninny would she be to wave to him like he was a knight heading to battle? He was going to talk to his father, and Kenneth Fortunado loved each of his six children and wanted their happiness above anything.

She only hoped Gavin's happiness wouldn't come at the expense of her heart.

"You look chipper today."

Gavin tried to wipe the grin off his face as he entered Maddie's office, which was currently occupied by their father. Kenneth sat behind the computer, a pair of wire-framed reading glasses perched on his nose. Although he'd officially retired last year, Kenneth was still in his prime and Gavin knew his dad was plenty capable of holding down the fort until Maddie and Zach returned.

One of the things Gavin missed most about living in Texas was spending time with his family. Despite occasionally wishing he were an only child, he truly loved being part of the Fortunado brood. His childhood had been idyllic, tons of love and laughter provided by the close bond his mother had fostered among all the siblings.

"It was nice to have everyone together for the wedding." He dropped into the chair across from the desk. "I also like seeing you in your natural habitat. Do you miss the daily grind of the agency?"

Kenneth smiled and shook his head. "I'm having a great time cheering on Maddie and Zach from the sidelines. It was one of my more genius moves to arrange for them to work together last year."

"Among a lifetime of genius moves," Gavin murmured with an exaggerated eye roll.

"Smart boy." His father steepled his fingers. "The smartest one remains marrying your mother. We're thrilled that Maddie's found so much happiness with Zach. It's what we want for each of our children." He raised a brow. "If you know what I mean?"

"As a matter of fact…" Gavin's stomach knotted even though his father had given him the perfect opening to discuss his relationship with Christine. He hadn't felt this nervous since he'd sat before his dad and explained that he was taking a position with a firm in Denver instead of the offer from one of his father's friends at a prominent Houston law firm. "I'm dating someone and thought—"

"That's wonderful, son." Kenneth's wide smile made guilt seep through Gavin's veins like poison. "Is it serious? Why didn't you bring her to the wedding?"

"Actually, it's serious and she was at the wedding." Gavin cleared his throat. "We've been keeping things private because she was worried about—"

"Worried?" Kenneth interrupted.

"About you," Gavin said softly. "What you'd think of our relationship."

"Why would I have a problem if she makes you happy?" He leaned forward, resting his elbows on the desk, the gold band on the third finger of his left hand shining. "Does she make you happy?"

Gavin thought about Christine's sweet smile and the way she looked at him like he was the only man in the world. "Yes," he murmured, almost more to himself than his father. "Christine makes me happy."

"Christine?" His father's expression went blank. "You're not talking about our Christine?"

"I am." Gavin drew in a deep breath as Kenneth frowned. "Although I wouldn't exactly say she belongs to the family."

"Would you say she belongs to you?"

Gavin thought about that then shook his head. "She's her own person. I like that about her." He held up a hand when his dad opened his mouth to speak. "But she's dedicated to you and to Fortunado Real Estate in general. Your approval of our relationship is important to her."

Kenneth inclined his head. "And you?"

"She's important to me," Gavin said immediately, surprised to find how much the statement resonated in his chest.

"Why haven't I heard about the two of you dating before now?"

"As I said, she wanted to keep things private at first to ensure it didn't impact her working relationship with anyone here."

"What's changed?"

Gavin fought the urge to grimace. It felt vaguely like facing a stiff cross-examination. "It's more than just dating, Dad. Christine and I are engaged."

"To be married?" his father asked, thick brows rising.

"That's the plan, and I'd like your support. You know I'm going to be spending the next few weeks in Austin. I don't want to have to hide anything or skulk around playing cloak and dagger if I want to see her. Plus, Schuyler is insisting Christine come to the reunion she's planning."

"I'm glad you talked to me," Kenneth said with a nod. "I don't like secrets."

Gavin chuckled. "Like discovering we're part of the famous Fortune family?"

"Some things even I can't control," his father admitted, almost reluctantly. "But you don't have to hide a relationship from us, son. I've told you we want your happiness above all."

Gavin didn't bother to explain how unhappy it made him that his family took such an interest in his love life. That feeling as though he were under the microscope had forced him into this arrangement with Christine in the first place.

But that wouldn't do any good at this point. Besides, he wasn't ready to end things before they even really got started. Pretending to be in love with and engaged to Christine might be a farce, but he liked her and knew they'd have a great time together over the next few weeks until he returned to Denver.

"Does that mean you approve?"

"You don't need my approval." His father smiled. "But of course I'm happy for you. Your mother will be, as well. You know how much we like Christine. Frankly, she's quite a step up in quality from the women you normally date."

Gavin rolled his eyes. "Schuyler said almost the same thing. I date decent women."

"Not in the same league as Christine."

"My girlfriends have been in Colorado," Gavin protested. "You haven't met most of them."

"Connor keeps us updated. He's ridiculously good with details."

"Connor should learn to keep his mouth shut. I'm not even sure he knows many of the women I've dated, so I'm not sure what makes him such an expert."

"He cares about you. We all do."

"I know."

"We care about Christine, too. Take care of her, Gavin. You aren't known for your staying power in relationships."

Ouch.

"Well, I'm committed to Christine now." Gavin smiled even as another wave of guilt crested inside him. His dad was right. Gavin didn't do long-term. It hadn't been a conscious decision, but he certainly had a habit of dating women who felt the same way about no-strings-attached as he did.

Christine was different. He knew that, even though their relationship was pretend. It was crucial he make sure they both remained on the same page so that she didn't get hurt.

"I'm glad to see it," his dad told him with a wide smile. "Your mom and I want you to be happy."

"Thanks, Dad. I *am* happy." He made a show of checking the Rolex that encircled his wrist. "I also need to get going. Christine and I are going to lunch."

"Enjoy," his dad answered, sounding pleased. "Let's plan a dinner with the two of you and your mom and me. I'm sure she'd be happy to come up from Houston to celebrate your engagement."

"Sure." Gavin walked toward the door. "I'll talk to Christine and we'll figure out a night that works."

"I'm really happy for you," Kenneth said, and Gavin left the office, trying to ignore the acid that felt like it was burning a hole in his stomach.

Chapter Six

Christine felt her smile falter as Gavin approached the reception area. He'd been sweet and flirty in her office earlier but now looked like a black cloud was following him. Had the conversation with his father gone badly? Was Kenneth angry that she and Gavin were supposedly dating?

"Lord, he's hot," came the appreciative whisper from behind Christine.

She looked over her shoulder toward Megan, the agency's young receptionist, who was staring at Gavin like he was the best thing on the menu at an all-you-can-eat buffet. "Um…yeah."

"Ready?"

She turned back to Gavin. "Sure. Is everything okay?"

"Fine," he snapped then closed his eyes for a moment. When he opened them again, the cloud had disappeared and a smile played at the corner of his mouth. He leaned in and kissed her cheek. "Don't mind me."

She heard Megan's gasp and felt color flood her cheeks. With a simple buss to the cheek, Gavin had effectively outed them to the entire agency. She knew that by the time they got back from lunch, everyone would know.

Maybe she'd order a drink with her meal. If only it was that easy.

"Be back in an hour," she said to the receptionist, purposely avoiding eye contact with the pretty brunette.

"I'll be waiting," came the reply. "We'll have a lot to talk about."

A drink couldn't hurt.

She and Gavin walked out into the hazy sun of the January afternoon, and she tightened the belt on her Burberry knockoff trench coat. She earned a decent salary with the agency but most of it went toward the monthly mortgage on her condo. She liked having a place to call her own more than she needed designer clothes.

"There's a new barbecue place a couple of blocks from here," she offered.

He stopped, inclined his head as if studying her. "I love barbecue."

Christine willed herself not to blush again. She wasn't about to admit she knew his taste in food from his sisters and from listening to stories of their family vacations over the years. That would make her seem like a total creeper.

"Me, too," she answered and started down the sidewalk in the direction of the popular restaurant.

Gavin fell into step beside her but didn't say anything more. When they stopped at a crosswalk, the silence became too much.

"Is your dad angry?" she asked, crossing her arms over her chest. "Does he hate the idea of the two of us? We don't have to do this. I mean, if it's—"

He reached out a finger and pressed it to her lips, effectively silencing her. She could barely remember to breathe when he touched her, let alone speak. "I'm sorry I've been quiet," he told her. "My dad is happy about our relationship."

The light changed and they began walking again. "Is there another problem?" she asked, glancing at him out of the corner of her eye.

"Everything's fine." He flashed a smile that didn't come anywhere near to his eyes.

Christine sighed. What now? Did she push him for the truth or let it slide? As much as she'd admired Gavin from afar for so many years, she didn't truly know him well. For all she knew, he had a toothache or had argued with his father about the Texans' chances in the playoffs this year.

They arrived at the restaurant, and he held the door open for her. She walked to the hostess stand and tried not to grimace as the woman looked between Christine and Gavin then did a double-take when he placed a hand on Christine's back, as though she couldn't imagine a man like him would be out with someone like her.

Sadly, Christine didn't blame the woman.

They followed the hostess to a table near the back of the crowded restaurant. Austin had plenty of barbecue joints but this was her favorite.

Christine made a show of studying the menu, almost disappointed when the waitress quickly took their orders.

She slipped the paper wrapper from her straw and tied it in a knot. As usual with this little ritual, the knot held when she made it but tore as she tightened it, and she sighed as the paper ripped.

When she glanced up, Gavin was smiling at her. "What's that about?"

She scrunched up her nose. "You never played the straw wrapper game?" She laughed when he frowned. "If the knot rips, someone is thinking about you. If not, you're out of luck."

"Yours tore off center," he pointed out.

"It always does."

"I'm thinking about you."

"You're sitting across from me," she said with a laugh.

"I thought about you all day yesterday," he continued. "About how much fun I had on Saturday night, especially the part where you curled against me in your sleep."

Her breath caught in her throat. "I don't remember that."

"You were asleep," he whispered and his voice took on a sexy edge.

"What exactly happened with your dad?" she blurted, somehow unable to let the subject go. "You haven't done a great job of convincing me he approves." Gavin's expression went from flirty to subdued in an instant. Way to ruin a moment, she chided herself.

At that moment the waitress brought their food. Gavin picked up his glass of iced tea, gripping it so hard his knuckles turned white. "He doesn't want me to hurt you."

"Oh," Christine breathed, knowing if she said anything more her voice would reveal that she shared the same fear.

"I don't want to hurt you," Gavin said, and somehow the words sounded like a promise. "I'm not going to hurt you," he added, almost like he was reassuring himself as much as her.

"Gavin." She reached across the table and placed a hand over his. He released his death grip on the glass and she saw his shoulders relax slightly. "We both know what this is," she said, even though it already meant so much more to her. "You aren't going to hurt me."

He nodded as if bolstered by her confidence. "I like you, Christine."

Warmth spread through her body at the simple pronouncement. "I like you, too."

"Do you think we could focus on that part?" He curled his big hand around her fingers. "We're friends who are getting to know each other better over these next few weeks. It doesn't have to be forced. I'm excited to hang out with you."

She swallowed. "You are?"

"Don't look so surprised," he said with a smile. "You're way more fun than you realize."

She laughed. "That might be the nicest thing anyone has ever said to me. I have a reputation for being organized, not fun."

"Then we'll work on your reputation."

She liked the sound of that.

"Is there anything else you need?"

Christine yanked away her hand and glanced up at

the hostess, who'd returned to the table in place of the waitress who had taken their order.

The raven-haired beauty was looking directly at Gavin as if he was the only one sitting at the table. "We're fine," he answered with a polite smile.

"Are you new to Austin?" the woman asked. "I haven't seen you in here before and I would have noticed."

Christine frowned as she picked up her chicken sandwich and took a bite. She couldn't believe the woman was flirting with Gavin right in front of her. Not that she could blame her. It was still almost difficult to look him in the eye some of the time. His gaze on her made her feel like her skin was on fire.

The hostess hooked two fingers in the waistband of her low-slung jeans, revealing the top edge of some kind of tattoo on her hip. She looked like she knew plenty about adventure and probably would have been friends with Christine's sister during high school. Certainly a woman who wouldn't have noticed Christine, unless she'd needed tutoring.

"I'm here for work," Gavin said, letting a bit of Texas drawl seep into his voice. "Originally from Houston."

"I could show you around," the woman offered with a sexy little half smile.

Christine figured if she tried that move she'd look like she was trying to hide something in her teeth.

Gavin returned the smile but gestured toward Christine. "I think we've got it covered."

The hostess's eyes widened. "You two are together?" She wagged one perfectly manicured nail between the two of them. "I thought she was your secretary."

"My fiancée," Gavin clarified without hesitation.

Christine drained her iced tea and held the glass out to the woman. "Could I get a refill?"

"Uh…sure." The woman took the glass and turned from the table.

"That was unexpected," Gavin murmured, digging into his own lunch.

Christine snorted. "You don't fool me. I bet women hit on you *all* the time."

"Not all the time."

She rolled her eyes. "Just on days that end in *y*?"

He grinned. "Something like that."

The hostess returned with the iced tea, placing the glass and a fresh straw on the table without a word and then walked away again.

Christine picked up the straw and pointed it at Gavin. "Why don't you have a girlfriend?"

"I was waiting for you," he said, making her laugh again.

"That's a bad line, even coming from your pretty lips."

He dabbed at one corner of his mouth with the napkin. "I've never been called pretty before. It suits me, I think."

"It's no wonder you became an attorney. You're such a smooth talker."

"I can't tell if that's a compliment or a criticism."

"An observation." She leaned in and repeated, "So why don't you have a girlfriend?"

He sighed. "You sound like one of my sisters."

"Which is not an answer to the question," she pointed out.

He studied her for a few long moments. "You do understand that I'm used to using my pretty mouth and fancy words to deflect questions I don't want to answer."

"I do."

"You're not going to let me get away with that?"

"I'm not," she said quietly. It might be the wrong thing to say. For all of Gavin's ease with people, she could tell he was a private man at heart. But she wanted to know that side of him, the part behind the handsome mask. Christine might not be the most adventurous or exciting person, but she knew how to be a good friend. She wanted to be Gavin's friend.

The waitress came to clear their plates, and Gavin gave her his credit card.

"Thank you for lunch," Christine said when the woman left again.

"My pleasure."

"Tell me about you and the lack of a girlfriend. Are you having trouble finding someone you connect with in Denver?"

He tapped a finger on his leather wallet. "I'm thirty years old," he said after a moment.

"Yes," she agreed. "Me, too. What does that have to do with dating?"

"At some point in the past couple of years, it changed. Expectations changed."

"Women got serious?"

"You could say that," he admitted. "Most of my friends got married. They settled down and bought real houses. Houses with yards in neighborhoods where you string up Christmas lights and build swing sets. Adult houses."

There was a thin note of panic in his voice, and she

wasn't sure whether to smile or roll her eyes again. "You're not exactly a 'failure to launch' type of guy."

"Being good at my job versus good as a husband and possibly a father are different things."

The waitress brought the bill, and after Gavin signed the receipt, they headed back toward the agency. A few clouds hung in the sky, and she was glad for her jacket to protect her against the brisk breeze blowing through downtown. Gavin didn't seem to notice the cool air, although that could be because he was used to winter in Colorado.

"You come from an amazing family," she told him.

He looked down and flashed a lopsided smile. "That's kind of the point. My dad is fantastic and my parents' marriage is as strong as ever. He always found time for each of his kids as well as my mom, despite how hard he worked. I know how to be an attorney, but that's nothing compared to being a husband or father. I don't know that I'm ready. I'm not sure I'll ever be ready. How could I compare to my father?" She noticed his hand clenched and unclenched at his side, a nervous gesture that was out of character for him.

This was it, Christine realized. This was Gavin behind the mask.

She reached out and took his hand in hers. "It's not a competition. Your parents want you to be happy, however that looks for you."

"I *am* happy," he insisted, squeezing her fingers. "I keep trying to tell them. I think maybe I wasn't cut out for more than what my life is now. I don't know how to admit that to anyone in my family. What if I don't have it in me to give more?"

At that moment a man burst from the crowd walking toward them, on his phone and clearly in a hurry, jostling people on either side. Before Christine could react, Gavin put an arm around her shoulder, tucked her to his side and shifted so that the man bumped into him instead of her.

Gavin didn't break stride or make an issue of it. He simply ensured that she wasn't bothered as he maneuvered them through the groups of working folks headed for lunch.

"You have plenty to give," she said, tipping up her head to look at the strong line of his jaw. She wanted to add that he just needed to meet the right woman. And maybe she could be that woman, but she didn't say those things because she couldn't bear to let herself believe they might be true. Despite his assurance, Christine understood that the only way to ensure Gavin wouldn't hurt her would be to not open her heart to him. A challenge, given how much she already felt.

They were almost to the agency office, so she started to pull away. Gavin didn't release his hold on her. He drew her into a quiet alcove between the buildings, turning to face her.

"When you say that, I almost believe it," he whispered. "I *want* to believe it."

"It's true."

She rose up on tiptoe to kiss his cheek, but he captured her mouth with his, his lips firm and smooth as they grazed over hers.

Her insides danced, electric sparks erupting along her spine. His tongue traced the seam of her lips and she opened for him, winding her hands around his neck and pressing closer.

Everything around her melted away as he deepened

the kiss. He made it too easy to forget that the only reason they were together was to appease his family. Christine hated that he had any question as to whether he could handle a real commitment. Even if their time together was temporary, at least she could spend the next few weeks proving that he was capable of opening himself to someone.

But right now all she wanted was to lose herself in this moment. And when he groaned softly, it was everything. She'd done that to him. A low whistle from the street had her pulling away.

"I can't... We shouldn't... This isn't the place."

He drew in an unsteady breath. "I'm sorry. You're right, of course. I just can't seem to control myself around you."

Now, *that* was definitely the nicest thing anyone had ever said to her. "I'm glad," she told him honestly, earning another smile. "But I do need to get back to work."

"Me, too." Then he leaned in and kissed her again. "When can I see you?"

"You're seeing me right now."

"A date," he clarified. "I want to spend time with you. We're friends. Remember?"

"Oh." She blinked. The way he was looking at her made her forget this was fake. "We could have dinner this week?"

"Perfect." He took her hand and led her back out into the street, stopping at the door of the agency. "Tomorrow night?"

"Okay." She swallowed. He wanted to see her again so soon, and not just because it was part of the charade.

She took a step away. "I'll see you tomorrow, then."

He kissed her one more time then walked toward the black SUV parked at the curb.

Christine straightened the collar of her jacket and then entered the office, shocked to find Megan along with two of the female agents staring at her from the waiting area.

"Gavin Fortunado?" Molly, one of the agents, practically hissed. "You've been holding out on us, girl. We want all the details of how you landed a fine man like that."

"He is so not your type," Megan said, shaking her head.

"How do you know my type?" Christine couldn't help but ask.

"I heard you were into Bobby."

Christine shook her head. "Only in his dreams."

"I told you so," Jenna, the other agent, said.

"Seriously." Molly took a step forward. "How long has this been going on with Gavin?"

Oh, no. Once again, she'd been so caught up in enjoying Gavin's company that she'd forgotten to clarify the details of their supposed relationship.

"A while. We're actually…" She cleared her throat. "Engaged."

"Are you joking?" Molly demanded. "How did you pull it off?"

Jenna swatted her on the arm. "You can't ask someone that."

"Come on, that man should be with a supermodel." She gestured toward Christine. "No offense. You're pretty but he's ah-may-zing."

"I know," Christine agreed immediately. She took a step forward. "I'll let you in on a little secret."

All three women leaned forward slightly.

"The way he looks isn't even the best part about him."

"Whatever," Megan said. "I'm not sure I'd be able to notice anything else."

Christine shrugged. "Then you'd be missing out."

There was a deep throat-clear, and all four of them turned to see Kenneth standing at the edge of the hallway. "Megan, could you pull our files on the Rosedale neighborhood? I want to compare comps for one of Maddie's clients looking at a house on Oakmont Blvd."

"Right away, Mr. Fortunado." The young woman scurried around to her computer.

"I'm meeting a client out in East Oak Hill," Jenna said quickly.

"I'm heading to an association meeting," Molly offered.

Christine noticed that none of them made eye contact with Kenneth. "Will you send me the listing information for the Hyde Park property when you get back?" she asked Jenna.

"Sure thing," the woman answered, her voice a nervous squeak.

Christine smiled as she approached Gavin's father and they walked toward her office together. "They're terrified of you," she said, patting his arm. "No one in Austin realizes you're just a big teddy bear on the inside."

He let out a low laugh. "Don't tell them."

"It's our secret," she agreed, turning into her office across the hall from the one Kenneth occupied this week.

"Speaking of secrets," he said in his deep baritone.

She schooled her features then turned. "Gavin spoke to you."

"You know you're already like one of my own daughters. Both Barbara and I feel that way. I'm thrilled that you'll be officially joining the family."

Emotion clogged Christine's throat as she nodded. Over the past decade working for Kenneth, she'd come to feel almost closer to him than she did her own dad. He never judged her for the things she wasn't but appreciated her for who she was.

"You never have to hide anything from me. I want you to be happy."

"Gavin makes me happy," she said, appreciating that she could give him a response that wasn't a lie. She suddenly had a clearer understanding of Gavin's mood earlier. It felt wrong to deceive Kenneth and the rest of the Fortunados.

At the wedding she'd acted impulsively, wanting to live out one of her secret fantasies and save Gavin from Schuyler's matchmaking in the process. But these weren't strangers whom she'd walk away from when Gavin returned to Denver and their relationship ended.

"I'm glad," Kenneth told her. "Barbara will be, too."

"I want you to know I'm still committed to the agency," she said quickly. "That won't change."

"I know." Kenneth frowned, his thick brows lowering over eyes that reminded her of Gavin. "I trust you implicitly, Christine. You just concentrate on staying happy, and I sure hope my son continues to be a part of that."

"He will," she whispered, somehow knowing Gavin would be the key to both her happiness and her heartbreak.

Chapter Seven

Gavin lifted his hand to knock on the door of Christine's condo the following evening, only to have it swing open.

"I can't go out with you," she whispered, her face pale and eyes wide.

He tightened his grip on the bouquet of roses he held. "Why? What's wrong?"

"It's Diana. She's sick." She took a step back, and he stepped into the condo. It was decorated in neutral colors but with colorful posters and pillows that gave it a homey look. Quite a bit different from the contemporary furnishings and unadorned walls of his loft in downtown Denver.

"Is Diana your daughter?" How had he missed the fact that Christine had a kid?

She gave him a funny look. "She's my dog."

He heard a low whine from the back of the condo, and Christine turned and started down the hall. She glanced over her shoulder at him. "I'm sorry. I'll call you tomorrow, okay? I've got to get her to the vet. They're staying open for me."

It was clearly a dismissal but Gavin wasn't about to walk away when she was so upset. He shut the front door and followed her into the kitchen, finding her kneeling next to a medium-size black lab that was on its side on the hardwood floor.

The dog looked up when he entered, gave a half-hearted bark then lowered her head to the floor again.

"What happened?"

"I'm not sure," Christine said, trying unsuccessfully to coax the dog to her feet. "Come on, Di. You can do it."

"I'll lift her," Gavin offered.

"She sheds," Christine told him, her voice hollow.

"It's fine. What kind of car do you have?"

"A Prius." She ran a trembling hand over the dog's head. "Normally, Di rides shotgun."

"We'll take mine. She'll be more comfortable in the cargo area. Do you have an extra blanket?" Gavin moved forward and knelt on the other side of the animal. "Hey, girl. Wanna go for a ride?" The dog's tail thumped as he pet her soft fur.

"You don't have to do this," Christine protested.

"I'm not leaving you."

He met her worried gaze, hating the panic in her eyes. "She's going to be okay," he said quietly, even though it was a promise he had no business making. But he would have told Christine anything at the moment to make her feel better.

She nodded and talked softly to the dog as Gavin scooped the lab into his arms. He straightened and started for the front door as Christine grabbed a blanket from the back of the sofa.

They got the dog into the back of his Audi SUV, and Christine told him which way to drive to get to the vet's office. Other than giving directions, she didn't speak, and he wasn't sure what else to say. He liked dogs well enough but couldn't begin to guess what had made hers sick. He reached across the console and took Christine's hand, wanting to offer whatever reassurance he could.

The vet's office was only a ten-minute drive from her place, and as she'd mentioned, the staff was waiting for the dog. The doctor, a gray-haired man in his midfifties, greeted both Christine and Diana by name as he instructed Gavin to follow him to the back of the clinic. Gavin placed Diana on one of the exam tables then returned to the waiting room and sat down next to Christine.

"I'm sorry," she whispered when they were alone. "This isn't your problem and—"

"I want to be here," he told her, lacing their fingers together. "I want to know you're okay. Tell me about Diana."

A hint of a smile curled her lips. "I adopted her from a shelter in Houston when she was only four months old. It was right after I started working for your dad. I'd graduated college and moved into my first apartment on my own so I wanted a dog for protection."

"How did she get the name Diana?"

"The shelter called her Princess. She'd been found as a stray. They don't know what happened to her mom or any other puppies from the litter. So I changed her name to Princess Diana."

He chuckled. "That's a funny name for a dog."

"Yeah," she agreed. "I might have entertained some girlish fantasies about my own Prince Charming back in the day. But despite the name, Di is so special. She was a holy terror when she was younger. Chewed everything she could get her teeth on. But it was love at first sight. We went for a walk tonight after work and she seemed fine. When I got out of the shower, she was on the floor." Her voice broke and she swiped at her cheeks. "I can't lose her. I don't understand what happened. I took her to the dog park after work, and she was acting a little out of it when we got home, almost like she was drunk. Then she settled down so I thought she was fine. Why didn't I realize something was wrong?"

"They'll figure it out," he assured her, wrapping an arm around her shoulder and pulling her close.

Normally, Gavin didn't do well with tears from women. Growing up in a house with three sisters, he'd seen plenty of crying in his day, but as an adult he steered clear of emotional scenes. Yet he couldn't imagine a place he'd rather be at the moment than at Christine's side.

She rested her head on his shoulder and they waited. Trying to distract her, he kept up a litany of questions about the dog, prompting her to share many of Princess Di's adventures over the years. Her love for the dog was evident as she spoke, and he hoped with everything inside him that the dog would recover.

The vet came out into the waiting room a few minutes later, studying a chart as he entered.

"How is she?" Christine leaned forward, clutching her hands tight in front of her.

"She's showing signs of poisoning, although I can't narrow down what could have caused it at this point. We've given her activated charcoal and IV fluids. You said on the phone she hadn't gotten into anything hazardous?"

Christine shook her head. "Unless it was something at the dog park that I didn't see. I've heard stories of dogs getting sick there recently but I didn't pay much attention."

The vet frowned. "It's possible, I suppose. Keep her on a leash for a while."

"So she'll be okay?"

The older man nodded. "We'd like to keep her here overnight. She should be ready to go home in the morning, assuming there are no complications."

"Can I see her?" Christine asked, her voice shaky.

"She's resting," the doctor answered gently. "It might be better if you wait until the morning. It's a good thing you got her here as quickly as you did."

Gavin frowned as Christine nodded. He could tell she was fighting back another round of tears.

They left the office, Christine's features a mask of pain. "I let this happen," she whispered as she climbed into the Audi.

"It's not your fault," Gavin assured her, squeezing her hands. "If some idiot put poisoned food at the dog park, there's nothing you could have done to prevent it."

"I was visiting with people while she ran around with the other dogs. I wasn't watching closely enough."

Gavin pulled the seat belt across her and fastened it. She was in no shape to take care of anything at the moment. It was painful to see Christine, who was always so quietly competent and capable, at a loss in this way.

"She's a dog at the park," he said, brushing the hair out of her face. "The whole point is to run around with other animals. The vet said she's going to be okay. It was smart that you brought her in for treatment right away."

She gave a small nod and leaned back against the seat, closing her eyes.

He got into the car and started back toward her house. They didn't speak during the short drive, but her breathing returned to normal and she seemed slightly calmer by the time he parked at the curb.

"Thank you," she said quietly, unbuckling her seat belt then turning to face him. "I'm sorry about the date." She shrugged. "Maybe we can take a rain check for later this week?"

"You aren't getting rid of me that easily." He turned off the SUV. "We can order pizza or whatever you want as takeout."

By the time he came around the front of the Audi, Christine was on the sidewalk. "I'm not great company tonight."

"Okay."

She threw up her hands. "Seriously, Gavin. You were such a huge help, but I'll be fine."

"*Seriously*, Christine." He reached out and brushed his thumb along the track of a tear that had dried on her cheek. "I wanted to hang out with you tonight. I still do. At least let me keep you company, since you're having a rough time. We don't even have to talk. Let's just eat and watch a movie."

"This isn't the night you planned."

"I planned to be with you," he answered simply and saw her draw in a sharp breath. "Let me stay."

She studied him for so long he felt himself wanting to fidget, but she finally nodded. "There's a pizza place around the corner. I have a menu inside."

"Pizza sounds great," he said, and taking her hand, they walked toward her condo.

By the time Christine finished her third piece of pizza, she felt almost human again. Maybe she should be embarrassed about her attachment to Princess Diana, but the dog had been a faithful companion and friend for ten years. She'd been a source of unconditional love and had seen Christine through several lousy boyfriends and always made her feel better about the strained relationship she had with her family. Everyone loved Di, even her unemotional father.

"She's going to be fine." Gavin repeated his words from earlier, as if reading her mind. She still couldn't believe how readily he'd pitched in to help with her dog and then comfort her. Sure, she could have managed, but it had been nice for once to feel like she wasn't alone.

"I know," she answered. "I just miss her. Other than when I'm away she's always with me at night." She thunked her palm against her forehead. "That sounds pathetically like my dog and I are codependent."

He flashed a grin. "Dogs are great. My roommate in college had a husky, and I loved hanging on the couch with that furry beast."

"You don't have any pets?" she asked, taking a sip from her second beer of the night.

"Nah. I like animals but I travel a decent amount. It doesn't seem fair."

"You could get a goldfish."

"I'll keep that in mind," he told her with a chuckle.

They cleaned up the dishes, empty beer bottles and the pizza box, and then moved to the sofa in her family room. "Are you sure you're okay with a boring night of television?"

"Being with you isn't boring," Gavin answered and the sincerity in his tone made her heart skip a beat. He sat close to her on the couch, and it felt natural to cuddle into him as they watched an action flick playing on one of the cable channels.

"Can I ask you a question?" His voice was a soft rumble against the top of her head.

"Sure."

"Why don't you have a boyfriend?"

She tried to stay relaxed but felt her body stiffen. Lifting her head from where it had been resting on his shoulder, she scooted away. "I haven't met the right guy," she answered, hoping that would be enough.

"I remember saying the exact same thing to you," he told her, raising a brow. "You didn't let me get away with it."

"But you're much kinder than me," she said hopefully.

He laughed. "Try again. When was the last time you were in a serious relationship?"

"I dated a guy in Houston for about two years, but we broke up before I moved back to Austin."

He whistled softly. "Two years is a long time."

She shrugged.

"What went wrong?"

"Well…" She took a deep breath and thought about

how to answer that question. "He wanted a schedule for…um…when we'd be together."

"When you'd go out?"

"When we'd *be* together." Color rushed to her cheeks. "In the biblical sense."

Gavin's eyes widened, and Christine wished for the ground to open up and swallow her whole. Why hadn't she just stuck to a vague version of the truth? They'd grown apart or wanted different things in life.

"He was a math teacher at a local community college, so logic and order were important to him. He created algorithms for our relationship and part of that was a schedule for the optimal timing of…you know."

"I know." Gavin nodded then quickly shook his head. "But I'm having trouble believing you."

"Maybe I shouldn't have made such a big deal about it," she said, echoing what her mother had said when Christine admitted to her the reason for the breakup. "I'm not exactly known to be adventurous. I've eaten the same type of cereal every day for breakfast for as long as I can remember. I'm not like you. My adventurous spirit is almost nonexistent. But that was too structured, even for me."

"Who says you aren't adventurous?" Gavin demanded softly.

She huffed out a harsh laugh. "No one needs to say it. Everyone knows it."

"I don't."

"You will," she countered. "You go heli-skiing and rock climbing and scuba diving." She held up a hand and ticked off their differences. "I'm scared of heights and speed and I can barely doggy paddle."

"There are other adventures you could have."

She wrapped her arms around her stomach and turned toward the television, hating the direction this conversation had taken. "At the end of the day, I'm a coward."

"I don't believe that."

"You're watching a boring movie with me and have dog fur stuck to your sweater." She rolled her eyes. "What's a typical date like for you in Denver?"

"Pretty similar," he said, deadpan. "Although sometimes I go for a crazy cat lady."

"I wish I knew how to let go and be wild."

Gavin leaned closer. "Do you have any memory of planting a mega kiss on me in front of my sister Saturday night?"

"Yes," she breathed.

He tipped up her chin and brushed his lips across hers. "That was not the work of a coward."

"It was different. I got swept away in the moment… in you."

"What's stopping you from doing that again? Every day, even?"

"Fear," she whispered, her eyes drifting closed.

She felt him smile against her mouth. "I love your honesty. There's no pretense with you."

"Too much talking," she told him, and deepened the kiss.

He let her take control, driving the intensity and pace. She pressed closer, and he lifted her into his arms. She ended up straddling him on the couch, loving the feel of his warmth beneath her. This was why it was a bad idea to schedule intimacy. The spontaneity of her connection with Gavin was one of the things that made it so special.

Well, that and the fact that it was Gavin under her. His big hands moved up her hips then under the hem of her sweatshirt, and she moaned when he skimmed his fingers along her spine.

"Lift your arms," he told her, and she automatically obeyed, too filled with need to bother being self-conscious. Her breasts were okay, she figured, and she'd at least had the forethought to wear a pretty bra tonight, preparing for all the possibilities before discovering Diana.

After tossing her shirt to the floor, he cupped her breasts in his hands then sighed with contentment. His thumbs grazed across her pebbled nipples, making heat pool low in her belly, but she wasn't going to be the only one half-undressed.

She pulled away from him and started undoing the buttons of his tailored shirt. He sat back against the couch cushions, seeming content to wait for her to finish.

When she did, he leaned forward so she could push the fabric off his shoulders. He shrugged out of the shirt then yanked the T-shirt he wore underneath over his head.

Christine thought for a moment that she'd died and gone to heaven. His body was absolute perfection. His shoulders were broad and his chest a wall of hard muscle. A smattering of golden hair covered his chest, and she splayed her hands over his bare skin, gratified when she felt his heart leap under her palm, and he groaned low in his throat.

He didn't try to hide that she affected him, even though she still had a hard time understanding why.

But now wasn't the time for second-guessing, not

with his touch driving her crazy with need. He leaned in and trailed kisses against the base of her throat, his hands snaking around her waist, pulling her up so that she was lifted to her knees. His hot mouth covered her breast and she moaned, threading her fingers through his hair as his tongue circled her nipple through the thin fabric of her bra.

It was too much and not enough at the same time. Christine wanted more, and as she had the other night, she forgot about being afraid or judged. All that filled her mind and heart was this man and how much he made her feel. How much she wanted to experience with him.

Then her phone rang, the sound like a bucket of icy water splashed over her head. She scrambled off his lap and reached for the device, which sat on the end table next to the sofa.

"Hello," she answered and then cleared her throat.

The overnight vet tech was on the other end of the line. As Christine listened, tears pricked the backs of her eyes.

"That's great news. Thanks for calling."

She disconnected the call and turned to Gavin. "Di just ate a bit of food and went out to do her business. She seems much better."

"She's definitely on the road to recovery."

"It sounds like it."

"I never doubted."

She nodded, then reached for her sweatshirt, suddenly self-conscious of sitting there in her bra.

"I should probably let you get some sleep tonight," Gavin told her, grabbing his T-shirt from the floor and shrugging into it.

Christine wanted to whimper in protest, both at him covering that amazing body and the thought of him leaving.

Of course, he was right. As much as she wanted to throw caution to the wind and rip all his clothes off, that would be the worst idea ever. The *best* worst idea ever.

"Thank you for tonight," she told him, standing and crossing her arms over her chest. "For dinner and your help and staying and…" Oh, Lord, she was babbling. She couldn't actually thank him for kissing her, could she?

"You aren't boring," he said as he buttoned his collared shirt. "Or a coward."

"Okay," she agreed, not wanting to talk about this. Hating that she'd admitted her fears to him. She had to remember to hold a piece of herself back; a lot of pieces, if she was smart. Because if she let Gavin all the way in, it would kill her when their time together ended.

"I had a great time being spontaneous with you," he said, his full lips curving at the corners.

That made her laugh. "Me, too."

"Will you text me tomorrow when you pick up Princess Di? I'd like to know how she's doing."

"I will," she said, and the fact that he cared about her sweet dog made her heart melt even more.

He took a step toward her, bent his head and kissed her. It felt like a promise of more, and Christine wanted all of it.

"Good night," he whispered. "Sweet dreams."

"Ya think?" she murmured without thinking, then blushed again as Gavin chuckled.

She locked the front door behind him, then straightened the condo and got ready for bed, missing Diana but comforted knowing the dog would be home tomorrow.

The happy glow Gavin had given her also gave a huge amount of comfort. And not just the crazy-good make-out session, although that had been…well…crazy-good. But his steady presence had made such a difference. Christine was used to doing things for herself. Even with past boyfriends, she'd remained steadfastly independent.

Her competence was her one inherent gift; at least that was how it felt growing up. She'd taken care of her family because that was the one way she knew to show love that they wouldn't refuse. It was unfamiliar to rely on someone else, and she would never have expected Gavin to be so easy to lean on for support. It made her goal of keeping her heart out of their arrangement even trickier.

But tonight she focused on how happy he made her. Wasn't she due for a little happiness?

Chapter Eight

By Friday Gavin's mood was as dark as the clouds that billowed across the sky above Austin, a harbinger of an impending thunderstorm. As much as he appreciated the predominantly sunny days in Colorado, sometimes he missed a good soaking rainfall.

Although not when the skies opened up as he parked two blocks from the restaurant where he was meeting Schuyler and Everett for lunch.

He dashed from his car toward the diner situated across from the Austin Commons complex, trying to stay under the awnings of the buildings he passed. Still, he was more than a little wet when he burst through the door. Schuyler waved to him from a table near the front, and both she and Everett grinned as he slipped into his seat.

"Where's your umbrella?" Schulyer asked, making a show of dabbing her napkin on the lapel of his suit coat.

"I don't own one," he admitted, making a mental note to find a store that sold umbrellas after lunch today.

"You've lived in Denver too long," Everett told him.

Gavin rolled his eyes. "I have an ice scraper."

His brother chuckled. "Not going to do you much good around here."

"I'll dry off eventually." Now that he was seated, he glanced around the diner's homey interior, appreciating the retro vibe of the decor. "What made you choose this place for lunch?"

"Best pie in town," Schuyler told him.

Everett nodded. "Lila wants me to bring her home a piece of lemon meringue. And cherry. And pecan."

"Wow." Schuyler glanced up from her menu. "I don't remember Lila having such a huge appetite."

"She's…uh…" Everett threw a look to Gavin then drew in a deep breath. "I'll share them with her."

"You could probably eat a whole pie on your own," Schuyler answered absently.

As he had at Maddie's wedding, Gavin wondered again if Lila and Everett might be expecting. But if his brother wanted to keep the news private for a while longer, he'd respect that.

"How's Christine?" Schuyler asked after the waitress had taken their orders.

"Fine." The truth was he hadn't spoken to Christine since he'd left her house earlier in the week. She'd texted him an update and photos of Princess Di, who seemed to be recovering nicely. While the dog was undeniably cute, Gavin had hoped for a little more. It was strange to find himself in this role reversal. Normally with women, he was the one trying to take things slow.

He'd learned early on in his dating life that if he didn't stay cognizant of managing expectations, he'd end up hurting women he cared about. So he'd established guidelines for himself around dating—how many times a week he could see a woman, the amount of phone calls or texts. Maybe it was cold, but he liked to think it had prevented heartache for his girlfriends and guilt for him.

Christine was different in so many ways. The romance might be pretend, despite their off-the-charts chemistry, but he liked spending time with her. An evening of a vet emergency, carryout pizza and an old movie had been the most fun he'd had in ages. He could be himself with her and wanted to make her see how much she underestimated herself. Gavin hoped their friendship would continue even after he returned to Denver, although the thought of moving into the "friend zone" and never kissing her again held no appeal whatsoever.

He'd expected her to call or reach out to him to let him know she wanted to see him again. That was how things usually went with women. He couldn't decide if Christine was playing it safe because of their arrangement or if she truly wasn't that interested in him outside of what was expected to maintain the ruse of being in love.

"Have you two thought any more about wedding plans now that you're in Austin?" Schuyler asked.

Gavin shrugged. "We're both busy."

"That's silly," she insisted. "Let me help."

"Schuyler could take care of everything," Everett added, none too helpfully in Gavin's opinion.

"Don't the two of you have enough of your own marital bliss to keep you occupied? How come everyone has so much time to worry about my love life?"

"We don't want you to mess it up," Schuyler said gently. "No one likes seeing you lonely."

Gavin felt the simple pronouncement like a sharp right to the jaw. "I'm not lonely. I have plenty of friends."

She shook her head then sipped at her water. "You have buddies to hang with and work colleagues. It's not the same."

Gavin darted a pleading glance at Everett. "Can you throw me a line here?"

"You have seemed at loose ends," Everett answered.

"Loose ends? How can you say that? I'm about to make partner."

Everett shrugged. "Having a good job isn't the same thing as having a good life."

"Coming from the man who was solely dedicated to his job until recently."

"Lila changed everything."

The waitress brought their food—a club sandwich for Schuyler and himself and a burger for Everett. As she placed the food in front of them, Gavin felt his frustration mount. This fake engagement with Christine was supposed to alleviate the pressure from his parents and siblings, not add to it. What would it take for them to get out of his business?

"I think it's great that the two of you are so happy," he said, forcing his tone to remain neutral. "Christine and I will start wedding plans when we're ready, but you have to trust that I can manage my own life. I'm not a kid who's going to make a stupid decision."

"Fair enough," Everett conceded, then took a big bite of his burger.

Schuyler looked less convinced. Despite the fact that she was one of the middle Fortunado siblings, she'd always been a caregiver for her brothers and sisters. Their mom found it amusing to watch Schuyler fuss like a mother hen, and Gavin knew she did it because she cared so much.

"You said you wanted to talk about the reunion," he told her.

She pointed a fry in his direction. "I'm going to let you change the subject because I love you. But know that we're all sticking our noses where they probably don't belong for the same reason. If you ever want to actually talk about your relationship with more than one-syllable answers to my questions, I'm here for you."

Gavin blew out a breath. Irritating as they could be, he loved his sisters and brothers with his whole heart. "I'll remember that. Thank you."

She smiled then popped the fry into her mouth. After she'd swallowed, she pulled out a pen and a small notebook from her purse. "I've confirmed with Nolan that his brothers and sisters will be there. They're flying in just for the party, so it will be a quick trip."

She flipped open the notebook. "The Paseo Fortunes aren't going to be able to make it because Grayson has some kind of rodeo award ceremony they're attending in Dallas. Nate promised they'd find another time to come to Austin to meet everyone."

"Lila heard that Gerald and the triplets' mom have rekindled their romance now that he's separated from Charlotte," Everett said between bites. "Obviously, it's a pretty big deal since Gerald and Charlotte were married for so many years. She can't be happy about losing him to his first love."

"Especially when she went to such great lengths to keep him from knowing about the triplets."

Gavin shook his head. When Schuyler first realized their connection to the famous Fortune clan, she'd traveled to the tiny town of Paseo, Texas, to talk to Nathan Fortune. Nate, along with his brothers Grayson and Jayden, were three of the illegitimate children of Gerald Fortune, who'd had a brief affair with their mother, Deborah, back when he'd been Jerome Fortune.

It was crazy to think that Jerome Fortune had been desperate enough to fake his own death and reemerge as Gerald Robinson as a way to escape his domineering father, Julius. And just as shocking to discover that their dad, Kenneth, was one of Julius's illegitimate sons, making them all Fortunes.

"Could you imagine Mom and Dad getting divorced at this point?" he asked his siblings, confident in his parents' love for each other.

"No," Schuyler answered immediately. "But I also couldn't imagine Mom trying to keep Dad from knowing he had three sons out in the world."

"Not just three sons," Gavin corrected. "Aren't there a bunch more illegitimate Fortune children out there?"

Everett nodded. "As far as the family knows, they've all been uncovered at this point. Apparently, Charlotte kept a secret dossier on each of them without Gerald's knowledge."

"It sounds like Gerald and Charlotte's marriage wasn't exactly perfect," Gavin said.

"Not at all," Schuyler agreed. "It still amazes me how open most of his legitimate kids have been about getting to know these half siblings. It's part of why I have such high hopes for the reunion. I really want all of us to feel like a family."

"Why is it important to you?" Gavin asked.

Schuyler was quiet for a moment before answering, "When I decided to infiltrate the Mendozas to get the goods on the Fortunes, I expected to be disappointed. Not only did I meet Carlo and fall in love, I also learned that the Fortune family is filled with a lot of decent people trying to make the best of difficult situations. I can't help but think that we have more in common with them than we might realize. Strength in numbers and all that."

Everett frowned. "As usual, it sounds like you've got everything figured out. Why do you need our help?"

"I'd like you to reach out to Gerald's sons. I know Ben and Keaton are willing to meet and I'm sure I can convince the sisters to attend, but I have a feeling the other brothers will respond better to a little 'mano a mano' talk."

"Don't you think Gerald's kids have enough to deal with right now?" Gavin took a long drink of iced tea. "First, all the illegitimate siblings showing up and then their parents separating? It's a lot to handle."

"But this is something positive," Schuyler insisted. "We're not a threat to them and neither are the New Orleans Fortunes. But we agree the Robinson siblings have handled all of the changes in their lives exceptionally well. I'm hoping they can help the rest of us."

"I'm willing to call Wes," Everett offered, mentioning Ben's twin.

Schuyler beamed at their eldest brother then turned her laser-focused gaze to Gavin. "What about you?"

"Big family parties make me itchy," he said, pretending to scratch at his arms and earning a fry in the face from his sister. "I'm more a lone-wolf type."

Everett let out a bark of laughter. "Not exactly spoken like a man who's ready for a trip down the aisle."

"I didn't mean it like that," Gavin amended, realizing he needed to watch what he said if he was going to make this fake engagement believable.

Schuyler seemed to take his comment in stride. "You can't spout that lone-wolf nonsense now that you're engaged to Christine. She's…" A wide smile split her lips as she glanced toward the door. "Speaking of your better half…" she said, wagging her brows at Gavin.

He turned to see Christine placing an umbrella in the stand next to the diner's entrance. She was with a woman he'd seen the other day at the agency office and the man who'd been hitting on her at Maddie's wedding.

His gaze narrowed as the guy leaned in to speak into Christine's ear. She laughed softly but shifted away, placing the other woman between her and her would-be suitor. Had the guy not heard she was dating Gavin? Was it possible he just didn't care?

As if sensing the weight of Gavin's gaze, Christine glanced toward him. His heart stuttered when she smiled as if the surprise of seeing him made her happy. Then her gaze flicked to Everett and Schuyler and he saw her draw in a sharp breath. She was nervous. He didn't want anything about their arrangement to make her nervous. She knew how much everyone in his family liked her. Although maybe that was part of it. She was afraid of what would happen when their time together ended.

He rose from the table at the same time she excused herself from her coworkers. The man—Bobby, if Gavin remembered correctly—gave Gavin a slow once-over then followed the other woman toward a table.

Christine walked toward Gavin and there was nothing fake or forced about taking her hand and brushing a lingering kiss across her mouth.

"Hi," he whispered against her lips.

"Hi," she breathed.

"Hey, Christine," Schuyler called from behind him. "Great to see you."

Gavin kept Christine's hand in his as he shifted so that she could speak to his sister and brother. It wasn't what he wanted. He wanted to pull her out of the restaurant and find a quiet place to reconnect with her, and if he was being totally honest, to kiss her senseless.

"Hey, Schuyler." Christine smiled. "Hi, Everett."

"How's the old man doing at the new office?" Everett asked with a wink. "Is he driving everyone crazy with his type-A personality?"

Gavin felt Christine stiffen next to him even though her smile remained fixed in place. "He's great, as usual."

Schuyler rolled her eyes. "Everyone probably feels like they're getting a break with him compared to Maddie and Zach. Those two are intense when it comes to real estate."

"We miss them, too," Christine said.

"Chris, we're ready to order. You coming over?"

Gavin felt his eyes narrow as Bobby called to Christine. "Who calls you Chris?" he muttered with a frown.

"Only my family and Bobby," she said. "I don't like the nickname."

"I don't like that guy," he said, dropping a quick kiss on the top of her head. "You can sit with us if you want."

"We're talking about the reunion I'm planning," Schuyler told her. "I'm so excited you'll be there, too. You're already like one of the family."

"Oh…uh…thanks." A blush rose to Christine's cheeks.

"Where's your ring?" Schuyler's gaze had zeroed

in on Christine's left hand. "I thought you'd be wearing it now that everyone knows about the two of you."

Gavin's stomach pitched. He hadn't thought about—

"It's at the jeweler being sized," Christine answered, squeezing his hand.

Schuyler nodded. "I can't wait to see it."

"It's beautiful," Christine said with a smile only he seemed to realize was fake. "I should go. Great to see you all."

Reluctantly, he let go of her hand. "I'll call you later?"

"Sure."

He leaned in to whisper in her ear, "And you'll answer?"

She nodded. "Of course."

"Great. I'm planning something for Sunday, so I hope you're free."

Her face went suddenly pale. "Sure. I guess."

Okay, that wasn't the response he'd expected, but he didn't want to push her for an explanation in front of his siblings.

He kissed her again, somewhat placated when she sighed and relaxed into him. That was more like it.

"Chris, come on."

"Can I punch that guy?" he asked in a tone low enough only she could hear.

"I don't think your dad would approve," she told him with a teasing smile before walking away.

"You've got it bad," Everett said when he sat down again.

"I'm ready for the wedding bells," Schuyler added in a singsong voice, then hummed a few bars of "Chapel of Love."

"You know Valene's still single?" Gavin grabbed a

fry from Schuyler's plate. "And Connor. I'm off the market so why don't you focus on one of them for a while?"

Everett chuckled. "You're such an easy target."

"Plus, you're only in Texas for a few weeks." Schuyler grinned at him. "Now that she's said yes, we've got to make sure you don't mess things up."

"I'm not going to mess up," Gavin said, pulling out his wallet when the waitress returned with the check. "Anything more we need to know about your reunion? I've got to get back to the office for a meeting."

As Schuyler went over details for the event, Gavin glanced behind him to the table where Christine sat with her coworkers. His gut clenched when she smiled at something the woman said. He didn't want to mess things up with her, but already their arrangement was more complicated than he'd ever imagined.

Mostly because of his feelings for her. She'd done him a favor as a friend by distracting Schuyler at the wedding and then agreeing to pose as his fiancée for his time in Austin.

It wasn't supposed to be more than that. He'd dated plenty of women and managed to keep his heart out of the mix with all of them. Why was Christine different?

She'd told him that she wasn't his type, and on the surface that might be true. But the connection he felt to her was undeniable. This crazy need to be near her made him both excited and anxious. He'd been joking when he made the crack about being a lone wolf, but it wasn't too far from the truth.

With her sweet smile and gentle spirit, it somehow felt like Christine was changing everything.

Chapter Nine

Either Gavin Fortunado had missed his calling as an actor or he was actually interested in her. Christine touched her fingertips to her lips when she was back in her office after lunch, imagining she could still feel the warmth of his mouth on hers.

Although she'd been a bundle of nerves running into him at the diner with Schuyler and Everett, he'd seemed relaxed and happy to see her. The way he'd taken her hand and then kissed her had made her feel like she was really his fiancée. But the rush of excitement brought on by that thought was followed almost immediately by a clenching in her heart.

If she let herself believe that, it could only end in heartache. When this started, she'd expected to put on a show when they were around his family. She would never have guessed she'd be going on actual dates with Gavin. And while she knew she should keep her walls up because of the risk to her heart, there was no way to deny how much she wanted to be with him.

She pulled her phone from her purse and dialed the familiar number.

"Christine?" Her mother picked up on the first ring. "What's wrong?"

"Nothing, Mom." Christine swallowed against the tension that accompanied every conversation with her mother. "I'm calling to say hi and see how you're doing."

"It's the middle of the day," Stephanie Briscoe pointed out as if she might not realize it. "Did you get fired?"

"No," Christine answered through clenched teeth.

"You said you were running the real estate agency those Fortunados own in Austin."

"I still am. It was a promotion."

"It sounds like a lot of work," her mother said drily. "I wasn't sure you'd be able to handle it."

"Mom." Christine sighed. How many times did she have to have some version of the "you can't handle your own life" conversation with her mother? "I've been working for Kenneth for ten years. I'm good at my job. They trust me. They rely on me."

"I worry," her mother whispered, indignation lacing her tone. "I'm your mother. That's *my* job."

"Okay," Christine agreed although her mother's concern had always felt more like judgment. "But I'm doing fine." She didn't mention the recent fall-off in business since the beginning of the year. In a meeting with Kenneth yesterday, they'd chalked it up to a normal post-holiday lull, but he hadn't seemed convinced and neither was she. Things had gotten off to a great start when Maddie and Zach had first taken over. She hated the fact that they'd be returning to trouble, even though it had nothing to do with Christine's role at the agency.

She wished she could mention the issues to her mother. It would be nice to have the kind of relationship where she went to her mom—or her dad, for that matter—for support and advice. But that wasn't the way of things and she didn't expect their family dynamic to change anytime soon.

"I'm glad," her mother answered. "I just want you to be okay."

"I know, Mom." She didn't bother to mention that it was the other Briscoe daughter who needed her mother's concern. Her sister, Aimee, had recently been fired from her job, and while she'd quickly been picked up by another salon, her spotty employment record was becoming a problem.

Christine had successfully graduated college and had a career she loved, but Aimee had floundered since high school, despite being a talented hairstylist. Their parents couldn't admit that the favorite daughter was the failure of the family, and Christine, whom no one had ever expected to amount to much, was thriving. She certainly wasn't going to point it out.

She decided instead to get to the real reason she'd phoned. "I'm calling about Sunday. I might not be able to make dinner."

"Christine, no. You promised when you moved back to Austin that you'd make an effort."

"I have," Christine insisted, hating being put on the defensive. "I've come for dinner every week."

"It's important to your father and me that the four of us spend more time together. Your sister is going through a rough time, and she needs our support."

Christine didn't want to hear about Aimee's rough time, which most likely stemmed from too many nights of partying with her friends and the monumental hangovers that seemed to prevent her from showing up to work on time.

"I understand, Mom. It's just one Sunday. I promise."

"Why can't you come?" her mother demanded. "Are you behind at work and need to catch up?"

"I have a date," Christine blurted.

Silence from the other end of the line.

"Since when?" Stephanie asked. "Who is this guy who wants to keep you from seeing your family? I don't like the sound of it."

Christine had to work not to growl into the phone. She loved her mother, but for some reason the love she received in return always manifested in criticism. It had been that way since she could remember. Her mother had constantly commented on Christine's weight or lack of friends, comparing her to Aimee with Christine always falling short.

"He's not trying to keep me from seeing you. I didn't mention it to him."

"Bring him to dinner," her mother answered simply.

"What?"

"You heard me. Unless it's some casual fling or you're worried we won't approve. I want to know more about your life, Christine. Let us meet your boyfriend. I want us to be closer. After the incident with my heart last year, you know I've been reevaluating things and focusing on what's important. You're important to me, sweetie."

Christine sighed. Just like that, all the fight went out of her. In addition to the position in Austin being a promotion, she'd taken the job to be closer to her family, and particularly her mother. Stephanie had a heart attack in March of last year, spending four days in the hospital then successfully completing months of cardiac rehab. Christine appreciated everything her mom was doing to make better choices in her life. She might not feel like she belonged in her adventurous, outgoing family, but she loved them.

In the hospital, her mother had told her she regretted that they hadn't been closer. She'd said she wanted another chance to repair her relationship with Christine. Wasn't that what every nonfavorite child wanted to hear from a parent, even as an adult?

"I'm not sure what time we're going out," she admitted. "But if it works, I'll bring Gavin to dinner."

"Gavin," her mother repeated, her tone gentler now. "I like that name. Does he make you happy?"

"Yes," Christine answered without hesitation. "So happy."

"Then I can't wait to meet him."

Christine said goodbye and disconnected the call. She'd purposely not mentioned Gavin's last name or that he was supposedly her fiancé. It was bad enough her mom would share with her dad and sister that Christine had a boyfriend. Christine still wasn't certain she'd have the nerve to take Gavin to Sunday dinner with her family, although the truth was he'd fit in better with them than she ever had.

She turned her attention back to her computer. Kenneth had tasked her with reviewing the agency's historical contract data to find a pattern to help determine why many of their deals were suddenly going south. It was worrisome but the task was something she could manage, unlike her feelings for Gavin.

Right now she needed to feel like she had control over something and it certainly wasn't going to be her wayward heart.

"We're doing what?" Christine felt her mouth go dry as she stared at Gavin.

"Ziplining," he repeated softly. "If you're up for it."

She concentrated on pulling air in and out of her lungs without hyperventilating. "Did you miss the part where I said I'm afraid of heights?"

He smiled.

"Deathly afraid," she added.

He took her hand and drew her closer. They stood in the area between her kitchen and family room on Sunday morning, light spilling in from the window above the sink. Gavin had arrived minutes earlier and looked even more handsome in a casual cotton button-down shirt and jeans than he did in his normal workweek uniform of a suit and tie. His hair was slightly rumpled and a thick shadow of stubble covered his jaw, like he hadn't bothered to shave for the entire weekend.

She was a big fan of this outdoorsy side of him.

Although not a fan of his plan for the day.

As if sensing her unease, Diana rose from her dog bed in the corner and trotted over for a gentle head butt.

"She can sense your fear," Gavin said, bending to scratch Di behind the ears just the way she liked. The animal promptly forgot about comforting Christine and melted into a puddle on the hardwood floor, exposing her belly for Gavin's attention.

"Traitor," Christine muttered.

"If you don't want to try it, we can do something else." Gavin glanced up as he rubbed the blissed-out dog's belly. "But you mentioned that you'd like to become more adventurous. The guy who runs the outfitter is a friend of mine from high school. I trust him implicitly so I figured this would be a safe way for you to face one of your fears."

"Safe," she repeated, testing the word on her tongue. How could she possibly be safe while harnessed to a cable and soaring through the air?

"I'll keep you safe," he said, straightening and looking into her eyes with so much sincerity that it took her breath away for an entirely different reason. A reason that made her knees go weak. "Do you trust me?"

She nodded, not convinced she could manage actual words at the moment.

One side of his mouth curved as if her answer made him happy.

"Are you ready for an adventure?" he asked.

She nodded again.

His smile widened. "I promise you'll be okay."

She said goodbye to Princess Di and followed Gavin out of the house, locking the door behind them.

When they'd gotten into his vehicle and turned onto the ramp for the interstate, he smiled at her. "How was your week?"

"Long," she admitted. "And busy."

"Maddie and Zach return later tonight, right?"

She nodded. "I'm glad they got away but it's too bad it was such a short honeymoon and they're coming back to—" She broke off, not sure how much to reveal about the drop in business at the agency.

"What's going on at the office? Is everything okay with Dad?"

"He's amazing as usual," she answered immediately. "Why do you ask?"

"You had a strange reaction when Everett asked about him in the diner the other day."

She shook her head. "It's not your dad. I'm not sure whether it's supposed to be a secret or not, but there have been some strange things happening with some of our deals lately."

"What kind of strange?"

"We're losing clients and having trouble with existing contracts. It doesn't make sense based on how strong business was right out of the gate. I'm not sure what's going on, but your dad's upset about it."

"Does Maddie know?"

"Not yet. It came to light this week, but there's definitely a pattern. Your dad didn't want to bother them while they were on their honeymoon. We're scheduled to meet to go over reports and trends tomorrow morning."

"She and Zach will figure it out," Gavin said, smoothing his thumb across the back of her hand. "There has to be an explanation."

"I hope so. We all had such high hopes for the Austin office." She stared out the window as the scenery changed from urban to more rural. It was one of the things she loved about Texas—the wide-open spaces. Even in the middle of the city, there was a sense of the cowboy spirit that made the state so special. Austin had a different vibe than Houston had, a more eclectic atmosphere with most folks taking the local slogan Keep Austin Weird quite seriously.

"Do you miss Denver?" she asked, glancing toward Gavin.

His fingers tightened slightly on the steering wheel. "I miss heading up to the mountains to ski on the weekends," he admitted. "Denver still has a bit of the cowboy feel to it, so it's not that different from Austin. A lot sunnier and less humid, I guess."

"My hair would love it." She tugged on the ends of her long locks. "Some days I'm a massive frizz ball no matter how much product I use."

"Your hair is amazing," he said. "The color is so bright."

She groaned softly. "They used to call me carrot top in school. I hated having red hair."

"It makes you special," he told her.

You make me special, she wanted to say but managed to keep her mouth shut. She'd told herself she would stay in the moment today and not worry about what might happen with Gavin or how much being with him made her heart happy.

Nope. She was keeping her heart out of the mix.

He exited the highway onto a two-lane road that led into the rolling hills north of the city.

"You doing okay?" Gavin squeezed her hand, and she hoped he didn't notice her sweaty palm.

"I can't believe I agreed to this." She leaned forward when the first zipline tower came into view, the seat belt stretching across her chest. "It's so high."

"You've got this," he assured her.

If only she had his confidence.

He parked in front of a cabin that seemed to be the outdoor company's office. Austin Zips read the sign above the covered porch.

Gavin got out of the Audi and walked around to her side. Her body felt weighted with lead, but she forced herself to climb out and pasted a smile on her face. "Looks like fun," she said, shading her eyes as she gazed up at the ropes course that had been built behind the office.

"Liar," Gavin whispered.

She laughed. "It's the stuff of my worst nightmares," she admitted. "But I'm going to face my fears."

Gavin leaned in to kiss her. "That's my girl."

"Fortunado!" A man's deep voice rang out from the door to the office.

"Hey, Marc," Gavin called. "Thanks for letting us come out on such short notice."

"It's our slow season," the man said as he walked forward. "But I'd always make time for you, buddy. I hear you're now one of the big-wig Fortunes."

Gavin's expression didn't change, but Christine felt a wave of tension roll through him. "You know how things go," he said casually. "It just means an even larger family."

"Sure," the man agreed affably. As he came down the steps, Christine couldn't help but smile. Gavin's friend could have been the Keep Austin Weird poster child. His sandy-blond hair was long enough to be held back in a man bun. Despite the temperatures hovering in the low fifties, he wore a pair of board shorts and a floral-print silk shirt like he should be hanging on a tropical beach instead of in the middle of nowhere outside Austin.

He shook Gavin's hand and did a couple of friendly back slaps then turned to Christine. "Gavin mentioned you have a bit of a fear of heights?"

She licked her lips and nodded.

"I want to reassure you," Marc said, leaning closer, "that you're in good hands with me. I've only had—" he tapped a tanned finger on his chin "—I guess that would be a half dozen equipment failures this year, but only one of them was fatal."

Christine took a step back. "Um…"

Marc threw back his head and laughed. "Joking with you, darlin'. We have a perfect safety record at Austin Zips."

"Right." Christine tried to laugh, but it sounded more like a croak. "Of course you do."

Gavin shook his head. "Not funny, Marc."

"Sorry." The man held up his hands, palms out. "We're going to make this easy and fun. By the time you're finished, you'll be shouting, 'More, Marc. Give me more.'"

Christine felt her eyes go wide.

"You seriously need to grow up," Gavin said, and his tone held a vague warning.

Marc seemed to get the message because he launched into an in-depth overview of the zip lines, the safety procedures and inspections that occurred each day and the standards his company followed to ensure a safe and fun experience for its customers.

Christine appreciated the information, and it gave her more confidence in Marc's level of professionalism.

"We're going to take the Mule out to the first platform. I have helmets and water already packed." He pointed to a four-seater utility terrain vehicle parked at the far side of the building. "You two load up while I grab my sunglasses and I'll be right out."

He jogged up the steps and into the building.

"You're going to be fine," Gavin said, wrapping an arm around her shoulder.

"Famous last words," she whispered, earning a chuckle from him.

"It's not too late to turn around. We can bag this whole idea and go see a movie or take Di for a walk. I'm just happy to have a day off and to spend it with you."

Christine appreciated the out, but she wasn't going to take it. "This is my chance to have an adventure." She flashed what she hoped was a confident smile as they got into the Mule with Gavin following. "Even if it's a miniadventure."

"The first of many," he told her.

The sun had warmed things enough to turn it into a perfect January day in Texas. She kept her focus on the blue sky and how nice it felt to be sitting so close to Gavin as Marc joined them and they headed across the rolling hills.

The zip line course was situated about a quarter mile from the building, traversing along the perimeter of the woods that bordered the property. As they got closer she realized the cables not only ran next to the woods but also through the trees, so that she'd actually have the sensation of soaring through the forest, if she could manage to keep her eyes open.

Marc parked then led them to the first platform. He gave another safety talk and explained how the two points of contact system with the safety lines worked. She and Gavin put on helmets and then the harnesses while Marc used his walkie-talkie to radio someone. A minute later an ATV sped toward them through the forest.

"This is Chip." Marc introduced an older man, who

was well over six feet tall and skinny as a rail. "He's going to be leading the two of you today and I'll follow."

Chip winked at Christine. "I'm going to go first down each run so you'll know it's safe."

She nodded then felt Gavin massage her shoulder. "You look a little pale," he said gently.

"Has anyone ever thrown up mid-zip line?" she asked Marc.

He laughed. "You'd be the first, darlin'. But don't worry about that. Do whatever's gonna make you feel better in the end."

"You've got this, Adventure Girl," Gavin told her as she clipped into the safety line then climbed onto the platform. Marc snapped Chip into the harness and with a playful wave, he took off across the huge open space between where they stood and the next platform.

"Wow," Christine whispered when Chip landed on the other side.

"Easy enough, right?" Marc asked.

Despite her racing heart and sweaty palms, she nodded.

He crooked a finger at her. "Do you want to go next?"

She shook her head. "Gavin will go."

"Are you sure?" Gavin asked.

"You need to be on the other end to catch me," she told him.

"I'll definitely catch you." He allowed Marc to connect his harness to the cable then took off, giving an enthusiastic whoop of delight as he sped from one platform to the next.

"I'd like to go home now," Christine whispered, earning a belly laugh from Marc. "Gavin made it look so easy. He's going to think I'm the biggest wuss in the world when I puke or pee myself on this harness. Could you imagine a worse way to end a date? I'm going to ruin everything."

"Darlin', I've known Gavin since we were stealing hootch from his daddy's liquor cabinet. I've seen lots of ladies on his arm over the years but never has he looked at one the way he looks at you. Don't worry about ruining anything. If you climbed down this platform and said all you want to do is go shopping at the nearest mall, that man would gladly hold your bags."

Christine smiled despite her fear. "I doubt that, but I appreciate you saying it."

"It's the truth."

"No shopping malls," she said, stepping forward. "I'm going to conquer my fear today."

"That's what we like to hear." Marc snapped her harness to the cable, explaining once again how to use the active brake if she felt she needed it.

Her knees trembled as she inched to the edge of the platform, and sweat beaded between her shoulder blades.

Gavin shouted words of encouragement, but she could barely make them out over the pounding in her head. She drew in a breath and took off, screaming first from terror and then with excitement as she sailed across the air toward the trees. She hit the brake lever the way Marc had shown her as she approached the next platform and a moment later Gavin's arms were around her. Good thing, too, because she wasn't sure she could stand on her own at the moment.

Chip unfastened her harness and she wrapped her shaking arms around Gavin's neck. "I did it," she whispered. "And I didn't pee myself."

Both men laughed and Chip patted her helmet. "Way to hold it together."

"You were amazing," Gavin said, kissing her cheek. "Are you ready to go again?"

She drew in a deep breath, most of her nervous butterflies replaced by exhilaration. "I am. Thank you for this day. It's the best ever."

He grinned and kissed her.

Marc joined them on the platform. "Okay, lovebirds. Let's hold off on the spit swapping until we're back to solid ground." He pointed at Christine. "Nice work. Next, we're going to show you how to curl into a ball to go faster."

The nerves returned, but Christine quickly tamped them down. She was going to try whatever Marc threw at her. The idea that she wasn't a total wimp made her feel braver than she ever could have imagined.

"I'm ready," she said, tightening the strap on her helmet. "For anything."

Gavin stood below the final platform, smiling as Christine rappelled down toward him, marveling at the change in her. As beautiful as she'd been at the start of their zip line adventure, there was something even more appealing about her now, a sense of abandonment that made her breathtaking. She was windblown with flushed cheeks and a smudge of dirt down the front of her shirt.

She hopped down the last few feet, grinning widely and doing a funny little dance with her upper body as Chip unstrapped the rock-climbing gear from her waist.

"She's a helluva sport," Marc said, handing Gavin a bottle of cold water. "I can't imagine bringing a woman who's deathly afraid of heights out here and having her handle it like a champ."

"She did great," Gavin agreed.

"You like her."

"She's extremely likable."

"Nah." Marc nudged his arm. "I mean, you really *like* her."

Gavin paused in the act of opening his water bottle. He hadn't mentioned the engagement to Marc. It was one thing with his family, but he figured it would be better to keep his story simple where he could. The pretend engagement definitely complicated things.

But he did really like Christine. Way more than he ever would have guessed at the beginning of their arrangement. Was that only a week ago?

How had his feelings changed so quickly?

"Where did the two of you meet?" Marc asked.

"She worked for my dad for years and now runs the Austin branch of the agency."

"So you thinking of moving back?"

Gavin felt himself frown. "My life's in Denver," he said quietly, suddenly understanding the point his siblings had been trying to make when they said a job was not the same thing as a life.

Marc slapped him gently on the back. "Not that I'm trying to skim your milk, but if the long-distance thing doesn't work out, I may have to swoop in to comfort her."

Gavin thought about the expiration date on their arrangement and his gut tightened. "No one's swooping in with Christine," he told his old friend.

Marc only laughed. "You've got it bad," he said, then walked forward to help Chip put away the equipment.

Christine grinned as she approached, pumping her fists in the air. "Did you see me?"

He smiled, pushing aside his discontent over the boundaries and timeline that defined their relationship.

"You were amazing." He wrapped his arms around her waist and lifted her off the ground. She smelled like a tantalizing mix of shampoo and the outdoors, fresh and clean. "Skydiving next?"

She laughed and kissed him. "Let's not get crazy."

When he lowered her to the ground, she cupped his cheeks in her palms. "Thank you, Gavin. I would never have done something like this on my own."

"I had no doubt you could."

Marc and Chip joined them and they rode back to the office. Christine laced her fingers with his like it was the most natural thing in the world, and damn, he wanted it to be.

"How about the ropes course?" Marc asked Christine with a wink. "It should be a piece of cake now that you're a master of heights."

Gavin expected her to decline, but she nodded and grinned at him. "Sounds great to me. What do you think?"

"Let's go," he told her and for the next hour they traversed the suspended ropes course, crossing bridges and climbing through obstacles. He could tell she was scared but never let that fear slow her down.

The sky was beginning to turn shades of pink and orange by the time they headed back toward Austin. Christine pulled out a pen and a small notebook from her purse and ticked off a list of other activities she wanted to try now that she knew she could overcome her fear of heights. Gavin's chest constricted as he listened to her plans.

He could see himself with her on every adventure, from bungee jumping to riding the roller coasters at the state fair. At the same time, he'd never imagined himself in a long-term relationship. Part of what allowed him to be so open with Christine was, ironically, knowing their time together had a built-in expiration date.

He could give himself fully because it was safe. But wanting more felt dangerous, both to him and to her. He didn't want to hurt her but his past had shown him that he wasn't the type of man who had more to give a woman like her.

"When did your fear of heights start?" he asked, needing to get out of his own head and the doubts swirling there. "You managed today like a pro."

Her grip tightened on the notebook. "My family went on a vacation when I was younger to a waterpark near Galveston. We were all supposed to go on this superhigh slide, but I didn't want to."

"Because of your fear?"

She tugged her bottom lip between her teeth. "Not exactly," she admitted after a moment. "I was overweight as a girl. It was a pretty big issue for my dad. He'd been a marine, and physical fitness was important to him. My younger sister was always into sports, and I never felt like I fit in. We're a year apart and as we got older, my dad started taking us on extreme vacations. I could never keep up so I think maybe I developed all my fears—heights, water and speed—as a way to have an excuse not to participate."

"So if you didn't participate, what happened?"

Her smile was sad. "The first couple of trips were

difficult because he'd try to force me to do things. Eventually, I just stayed behind with my grandma."

"While your family went on vacation without you?"

"It wasn't a big deal," she insisted. "In fact, I had a much better time with my grammy than I would have if I'd tried to keep up with the rest of them."

"Christine—"

"Anyway, that's how it started." She gave him a smile that was as bright and brittle as a piece of cut glass. "But today changed everything. Thank you."

"You don't have to thank me. I'm glad I could be there with you. Now, what are you thinking for dinner?"

She sucked in a breath and glanced at the clock on the Audi's dashboard. "Oh, no. Is it really after five?"

He nodded. "Time flies and all that."

"I'm supposed to be at my parents' for dinner by six. It felt like we zip-lined for thirty minutes."

"More like three hours plus time for the ropes course. Where do your parents live?"

"On the west side of Austin, near West Lake Hills."

"I could—"

"They want you to come, too," she blurted then covered her face with her hands. "I'm sorry. I should have said something earlier. I tried to get out of the dinner, but I told you my mom thinks that Sunday dinners with the four of us will somehow bring us closer."

"I don't—"

"I'm sure it sounds horrible," she continued, shifting her hands to glance at him from the corner of her eye. "I don't blame you for not wanting to go. But it's out of the way to go all the way back to my place. If you just drop me off at my parents' now, after dinner I can call an Ub—"

"I don't mind going," he interrupted, reaching out to tug her hands away from her face. "I'd like to meet your family."

She wrinkled her nose. "Why?"

"Because I want to know you better," he said with a laugh. "You know my family, and they all love you."

"My family is different from yours, and not in a good way."

"It doesn't matter."

"There's nothing to learn about me from meeting them."

"If your mom wants me there, I don't want to rebuff the invitation."

"Are you sure?" She sounded even more nervous than she'd been before the zip line tour. "I can make an excuse. This definitely wasn't part of our arrangement."

"I'd like to join you for dinner with your parents and sister," he said gently. "But only if you're okay with it. If not, I'll drop you off around the corner then come back and pick you up when you're ready to leave."

"Seriously?" she couldn't help but ask. "You'd do that for me?"

Gavin was quickly coming to realize he'd do just about anything for this woman, but he wasn't about to admit it out loud.

"That's what friends are for," he answered instead.

Chapter Ten

Christine tried not to look like she was about to throw up as she opened the door to her parents' house and led Gavin inside.

At this point she would have taken skydiving, maybe even without a parachute, over introducing him to her family. The prospect of it had seemed manageable during the drive, thanks to Gavin's quiet confidence, but the reality of it was a different story.

"Chris?" her mom called from the kitchen, and she grimaced. She hated the nickname her family still insisted on using. It brought back memories of being a chubby kid with an unfortunate bowl haircut that made her look like a boy. She'd tried her hardest to fit in but ended up feeling lousy about herself most of the time.

She wanted to believe she'd shed her self-doubts the way she had her extra weight, but it was easier when she was away from this house and her family.

"Hi, Mom," she said with a forced smile as she entered the kitchen.

Her mother looked up from where she was cutting tomatoes for a salad, her eyes widening at the sight of Gavin. Christine might not be the fat, awkward girl she once was, but she knew her mom wouldn't expect her to be dating someone who looked like Gavin.

Christine's dad walked into the kitchen from the family room. "Hey, kid," he said, taking in Christine's tousled hair and dusty clothes. "Looks like you need a shower."

"We went zip lining and didn't have time to change before coming here," she reported. "Mom and Dad, this is Gavin Fortunado. My…um…boyfriend." Cursing her fair complexion, she willed away the color she could feel flooding her cheeks. She hoped Gavin was okay that she didn't mention their pretend engagement to her family. She understood why it helped with the Fortunados, but the shock of her having an actual boyfriend would be plenty for her parents and sister.

"Fortunado? Like the family who owns the agency where Christine works?"

Gavin nodded. "Kenneth is my dad. Christine and I met at the office in Houston."

"I'm Stephanie and this is Dave," her mother told him, her tone almost dazed. "Are you a real estate agent?"

"Nice to meet you," Gavin said smoothly, walking forward and shaking first her father's hand and then her mother's. "I'm actually an attorney, and I'm sorry Christine and I are a bit of a mess. She just had to do the ropes course after we finished the zip line tour, and time got away from us."

Dave Briscoe gave a disbelieving laugh. "Chris on a ropes course? You've got to be kidding."

"I'm not." Gavin pulled out his phone. "She did fantastic. Would you like to see the photos?"

Her mother put down the knife. "I would."

"Did they have a harness big enough for her?"

The comment came from behind her and Christine turned, her chest tightening as her sister, Aimee, sauntered into the room. She wore a black tank top and tight jeans that hugged her trim hips. Aimee placed an empty beer bottle on the counter and gave a bubbly laugh, like this was all a big joke. "Oh, wait. She's not fat anymore. I always forget."

"I lost the weight years ago," Christine said through clenched teeth.

Gavin gave her sister the barest hint of a smile then took out his phone and pulled up the photos for her mother.

"Good for you, Christine," her mom said, taking the phone from Gavin and scrolling through the photos. "You don't look scared at all. Dave, look at these pictures."

"It was fun," Christine said quietly, darting a glance at her sister. Historically, Aimee did not respond well to Christine getting attention from their mother.

"Do you live in Austin, Gavin?" She moved around the counter, tugging on the hem of her tank top, revealing more of her world-class cleavage.

Christine glanced at Gavin, but he didn't seem to notice. How was that even possible?

"Denver," he answered. "I'm in Austin for a few weeks because of work."

"Do you ski?"

"Whenever I get the chance."

"I'm road-tripping up to Vail with some friends next month. I just ordered a new set of twin tips."

"Sounds great," he said, but shifted closer to Christine.

She tried to take comfort in his presence but couldn't seem to settle her nerves. "Aimee, Mom said you lost your job."

"I got another one," Aimee snapped. "A better one." She turned to Gavin. "We're looking to do the back bowls. Expert terrain only. You should meet us up there. It's an awesome group."

"Thanks for the invite," he said.

"Chris doesn't ski," Aimee announced as if Christine had tried to make Gavin believe that she did. "There's no way she'd be able to handle even the bunny hill." She laughed again. "Don't even get me started on a chairlift. With her fear of heights—"

"You should take a look at the photos," Gavin told Aimee as Christine's father handed back his phone. "She's got that fear of heights under control."

Christine glanced toward her father, who was studying her like he'd never seen her before. It had been so easy to believe she'd conquered the worst of her fears when they'd been in the middle of their date. Now she felt as awkward and bumbling as she always had with her family.

"It's nice to see you smiling," Dave said finally, inclining his head toward Gavin's phone.

Not exactly a ringing show of support but it felt like a huge endorsement from her normally recalcitrant father. Aimee must have noticed it, too, because her eyes turned hard.

"Let me show you my workshop while the women finish up dinner," Dave told Gavin. "Got a beer cooler out there stocked with cold ones."

Gavin nodded but looked at Christine's mom. "Do you need help with anything?"

Christine watched her mother's face soften. Her parents loved each other, but theirs was a traditional marriage with the bulk of the household duties falling to Stephanie. She could tell it meant a lot to her mom that Gavin offered to help. Once again Christine reminded herself that today was merely a detour on the trajectory of their relationship, which couldn't end in anything but heartache for her. How much of her heart she gave him was the only question.

"Thank you for the offer," her mom said, blushing slightly. "But I've got things under control. Dave is so proud of his workshop. You go with him."

"I'd love a beer, then," Gavin said to her dad and followed Dave toward the garage that housed his workshop.

"He's so handsome," her mom said when the door closed behind the two men. She fanned a hand in front of her face. "Makes me feel like I'm having a hot flash."

Christine knew exactly how her mother felt.

"It's difficult to believe you landed someone like him," Aimee said, opening the refrigerator to pull out another beer. The workshop was their father's man cave and a space where Christine's mother rarely ventured. Instead, she kept a few beers stocked in the kitchen fridge for when friends or her daughters stopped by. Of course, Aimee didn't bother to offer one to Christine now.

"He's great," Christine murmured, hoping to avoid

an in-depth conversation about Gavin. The Briscoe women might not be close, but she feared that her mom and sister would be able to read the lie of their relationship on her face nonetheless.

"What's he doing with you?" Aimee asked as she popped the top on the beer bottle.

"Be nice," their mother chided.

"We have a lot in common," Christine said, automatically going to the cabinet to begin setting the table. It was the second Sunday of the month, so that meant meat loaf. She could smell it baking, and the scent brought back both good and bad memories from childhood. Her mother had always been a great cook, although it still embarrassed Christine to remember herself as a girl, trying to take an extra portion at mealtimes or sneaking into the kitchen late at night to munch on leftovers.

Aimee took the napkins out of the drawer and followed Christine to the table. "Like what?"

How was she supposed to explain her connection to Gavin? On the surface, they were a mismatched pair, but he seemed to like her just the way she was. She saw beyond his polished playboy facade to the kindhearted man he didn't reveal to many people. That sort of connection would be lost on her abrasive sister, most likely chalked up to wishful thinking on Christine's part.

"Well, we both like zip lining." She grinned when Aimee snorted. "I'm also going to learn to water-ski this summer." Gavin gave her the confidence to conquer her fears. She'd never been a strong swimmer, mostly because as a kid she hadn't wanted to be seen in a bathing suit. But she could start doing laps in the pool at the gym where she belonged. By summer, certainly she'd be ready for waterskiing.

"Is Prince Fortunado going to teach you?" Aimee asked, her tone at once bitter and teasing.

"Maybe." Christine bit down on her lip. On second thought, Gavin probably wouldn't be around to see her water-ski, if she even managed it. Aimee didn't need to know that. She placed a plate at the head of the table and glanced up to meet her sister's gaze. "Or you could help me. I remember how great you were when we'd go out to Aunt Celia's place in the summer."

"That's a lovely idea," their mother said, clapping her hands together. "I'd love to see you girls doing something together."

Aimee looked torn between shooting down Christine and placating their mother. "If I have time," she agreed eventually. "We'll see."

Christine smiled even as her stomach pinched. She wished she understood where the animosity between the two of them had originated. Their parents loved them both, although Dave Briscoe had made it clear that he wished he'd had a son. Aimee had done her best to fill that void by being a rough-and-tumble tomboy growing up, interested in sports and cars and whatever else she thought would bring her closer to their father.

Christine had been the odd one out, so Aimee's constant resentment didn't make sense, but it had persisted just the same.

Maybe it was silly that she still wanted a relationship with her sister, but she couldn't help it.

"It's obvious Gavin really likes you," Stephanie said, ignoring her younger daughter. "I like seeing you this happy."

"Thanks, Mom."

Aimee grumbled a bit more but they managed to get

dinner on the table without an outright argument. Christine's father was more animated than she'd seen him in years during the meal. It was clear he liked Gavin, and Christine felt the all-too-familiar guilt that she was exposing her family to their fake relationship. Obviously, her parents would be sorely disappointed when she and Gavin parted ways. But she consoled herself with the knowledge that at least now they saw her as more than just their boring, awkward daughter.

Thanks to Gavin, she felt like so much more.

She made an excuse about needing to prepare for a Monday meeting, and they said their goodbyes soon after dinner. The sun had fully set while they were at her parents' and she was grateful for the cover of darkness so she had a bit of time to regain control of her emotions.

The ride back to her house was quiet, and she wasn't sure what to make of Gavin's silence. Her family and her role in it were the polar opposite of the tight-knit Fortunado clan. Even discovering the connection to the famous Fortunes had only seemed to bring them closer. She couldn't imagine anything that would truly bridge the distance in her family.

When he pulled up in front of her condo, she pasted on a smile and turned to say good-night, only to have him lean across the front seat and fuse his mouth to hers.

Her breath caught in her lungs, and she immediately relaxed into the kiss even though the intensity of it shocked her.

"That was fun," he whispered against her lips.

She pulled back with a soft laugh. "You must be talking about the kiss because dinner with my family was about as much fun as a root canal."

"They don't give you enough credit," he said, his tone serious.

She shrugged. "It's hard to break old patterns. You wouldn't understand because your family is perfect."

"Hardly," he answered with a snort. "I don't think any family is perfect."

They both looked out the front window as headlights turned down the street, illuminating the front of the Audi. "I need to take Princess Di for a walk," she said, her heart suddenly beginning to pound in her chest. "Any chance you want to join me?" It was such a simple question, yet it felt funny requesting something from Gavin. He had initiated most of the time they'd spent together, and it felt strange to be so nervous—like somehow she was imposing on his evening.

He flashed a small, almost grateful smile. "I'd love to."

They walked to her condo hand in hand, and she unlocked the door, immediately greeted by the dog. While Gavin got busy loving up Diana, Christine pulled on a heavier jacket and took the dog's leash from its hook in the laundry room. She grabbed a flashlight, as well, and they headed out to the street.

"My family sometimes feels larger than life," Gavin said as they walked, Princess Di happily sniffing the edge of the sidewalk as she trotted along. "We all have big personalities."

"It's one of the things I liked best when I first started with Fortunado Real Estate," Christine admitted. "Your dad is great and it was fun when any of the kids or your mom stopped by the office."

"Yeah. We're a ton of fun." Gavin scrubbed a hand across his jaw, the scratchy sound reverberating in the quiet of the evening and doing funny things to Christine's insides. "But growing up it was hard to get noticed—there were so many of us doing different activities. Honestly, my mom is a saint for handling all of it. But that's part of how I became an adrenaline junkie. All of my antics were a way to get attention."

"Really?" Christine was shocked by the admission. "The adventurous side of you seems so natural."

He shrugged. "I guess it is by this point, but sometimes it feels like a compulsion rather than something I do because I love it. Don't get me wrong, I like to have fun, but I wonder if there's more to me than working and taking off on the weekend for more thrill-seeking."

"I think there is," she said softly.

"I don't even own a houseplant," he told her out of nowhere.

She frowned. "Um…okay."

"I know that sounds random." He shook his head. "But I'm not exactly known for my skills at adulting. I have a great job, but even at the firm I'm the guy who woos the prospective clients. I move too fast to be able to stay with one for the long haul, so much that it's a shock I'm in Austin for so long. I admire your dedication and how steady you are."

"Thank you," she whispered.

"And your sweetness and loyalty," he continued. As the dog blissfully investigated a nearby shrub, Gavin turned and cupped her cheeks between his palms. "Your family doesn't have any idea how lucky they are to have you."

She swallowed the emotion that threatened to clog

her throat. She wanted to believe that. It didn't matter that she was a grown woman and had made a wonderful life for herself. The fact that she'd never fit in with her parents and sister was like an itch that she couldn't seem to scratch, always distracting her from allowing herself to be truly happy.

"I'm lucky to have you," he continued, and her heart soared. "Even if it's only for a few weeks, I'm grateful for our time together."

Right. Like a balloon that had been stuck with a pin, her happiness deflated, thanks to the reminder that their arrangement was temporary. Gavin might enjoy being with her, but he wasn't looking to make this into something real. He had no problem remembering the parameters of their relationship. Why did she?

"We should head back," she said, pulling away and tugging on Di's leash. "I actually do have a meeting first thing tomorrow with Maddie and Zach."

He frowned but dropped his hands. The cool night air swirled around her, making her body miss the warmth of his touch.

She purposely kept a greater distance between them as they returned to her condo. What was the point of letting him close when he was just going to walk away? She might not be the most confident woman in the world, but she had enough self-respect to not allow herself to turn into a blathering idiot begging him to want more. At least not to his face.

"Can I see you this week?" he asked, placing a hand on her back as she unlocked her door.

Whenever you want, her heart shouted. It felt like her emotions were rattling her insides like bars on a prison window. What would happen if she threw her self-respect to the wind and invited him in? Would he take her up on the invitation?

Instead, she smiled and shook her head. Physical distance was the only way she could think of to keep her feelings for him from spiraling out of control. "It's going to be crazy around the agency with your sister and Zach returning. I think it would be better if we waited until the reunion next weekend."

"Oh." Gavin's thick brows drew together over his gorgeous green eyes. "Is everything okay?"

I'm falling for you, she wanted to tell him. *I don't know how to stop it or protect my heart.*

But she did know and, unfortunately, it involved keeping her distance unless they had to be together for the ruse. She hated pushing him away, but what choice did she have?

"Everything's fine, but I'm busy and I'm sure you are, too. I mean, the sooner you close the new client, the sooner you'll be able to head home. Right?"

"I guess," he said slowly. "I'm in no hurry."

"Me neither," she admitted before she could stop herself. Princess Di gave a soft whine, ready to be in bed for the night. "Let's talk in a few days," she told Gavin with fake cheer. "Thanks again for the adventure, and for joining my family for Sunday dinner—an adventure unto itself."

He stepped back, studying her face as if trying to figure out why she was acting so remote. She couldn't explain it to him, couldn't bear for him to deny that he would hurt her.

Already her heart ached more than she could have imagined.

"Good night," she said and slipped into her quiet house.

Chapter Eleven

Gavin tugged on the collar of his crisp white shirt as he approached Christine's front door Saturday night. He hadn't been this nervous about a date since…well, he'd never been this nervous.

Other than a couple of awkward phone conversations and a few random texts, he hadn't spoken to her since the previous Sunday evening. He wasn't sure what went wrong. They'd had a perfect day, even if the visit to her parents' had been a tad uncomfortable.

Actually, the new understanding of the role Christine played in her family made him furious. Beyond her dedication to his father and the family business, Christine was an amazing person in her own right. Maybe he hadn't noticed her understated beauty and charm at first—or in the ten years he'd known her. But now that he'd spent time with her he couldn't envision his life without her sweetness and light in it.

Except that was exactly what was going to happen at the end of the month. He'd mentioned the predetermined finish to their arrangement, hoping to coax some sort of reaction from her, but she hadn't batted an eye. Not that he blamed her. He'd all but told her he was a bad bet for a relationship. Why wouldn't he expect her to take him at his word?

In fact, her mood seemed to change after he revealed his feelings about his own childhood, the ones that left him riddled with guilt for being an ungrateful schmuck. His family was fantastic and what did it matter if he had to work to be noticed in the midst of so much love? But he'd gotten so used to pushing himself for the rush of adrenaline that he didn't know any other way to live.

Yet with Christine it was easy to slow down and enjoy the moment, whether walking her dog or watching her conquer her fears. She made everything a little brighter, helped him breathe easier than he could ever remember.

He'd gotten himself onto a crazy treadmill of working hard and playing hard, a cliché overachiever in every area except the one that counted the most—his personal life. He'd always doubted he had the capacity for the kind of love his parents had, the kind Everett, Schuyler and Maddie had found. As crazy as it was and despite the unexpected way their connection had come about, he saw that potential with Christine. And now he doubted she'd give him a chance to prove it.

He knocked, smiling as Princess Di gave a loud *woof* on the other side of the door.

"I'm ready," Christine said as she opened it.

Gavin started to smile then felt his jaw go slack.

"Wow," he murmured as he took her in.

"Is this dress okay?" She smoothed a hand over the front of the soft fabric. The dress was black and strapless with a thin sash around the waist and fell to just above her knees. She'd paired it with a delicate gold necklace, dangling earrings and a pair of the sexiest heels he'd ever seen. This was a Christine he hadn't seen before. Her hair was swept to one side and fell in soft waves over her bare shoulder. His fingers itched to touch it, to touch her. He wanted to pull her close and hold on all night. "Schuyler said cocktail attire, but I don't want to seem overdressed."

"You're perfect." He shook his head, his brain jumbled as if he were the ball in an arcade pinball machine. "So damn beautiful."

She laughed and a blush stained her cheeks. He'd missed seeing that rosy glow. He'd missed her so much it made him feel like a fool. It had been six days. Barely any time at all and yet...

He leaned closer, breathing in the delicate scent of her.

"What are you doing?" she asked with a laugh, taking a step back into her condo.

"Making sure you hadn't changed shampoos since I saw you last."

"You're crazy," she told him.

"For you," he confirmed.

Di nudged Christine's legs, trying to reach Gavin. "Hey, girl," he said, bending to scratch behind the dog's furry ears. "I missed you, too."

"Gavin." Christine's tone was serious. He frowned as he straightened, wondering what he'd done wrong now.

"Yes?"

"You look nice, too," she said, almost shyly.

He swayed closer, ready to meld his mouth to hers,

but she turned away, grabbing her purse from the entry table. "We don't want to be late. Schuyler wants the family there before the New Orleans Fortunes are scheduled to arrive at four."

"There's plenty of Fortunados to handle the welcome." He moved closer, crowding her a little. Her breath hitched and it gave him so much satisfaction to know she wasn't as unaffected by him as she acted.

"It's important," she insisted.

He sighed. "You're right, of course."

"Of course."

"First, I have something for you." He pulled a small velvet pouch from the inside pocket of his suit jacket.

Her mouth formed a small O as she watched him take a six-prong diamond solitaire engagement ring from the pouch. "I think you need to be wearing a ring when we get to the reunion."

"Yes," she breathed then pressed two fingers to her lips. "I mean, you're right. You didn't actually ask me anything." She stared at the ring. "But, yes, just the same."

It made him ridiculously happy to hear her say yes. He slipped the ring onto her finger. "It's on loan from one of the firm's clients who owns a chain of jewelry stores throughout Texas."

"A loan," she whispered, seemingly unable to pull her gaze from the sparkling diamond. "You have some darn good connections."

"Thank you again for doing this, Christine."

"Of course." Her gaze lifted to his as she closed her left hand into a tight fist. "We should really get going."

He stepped back so she had room to close the door and resisted the urge to take her hand as they walked toward the Audi. Clearly, he'd spooked her last week with something he'd said or done. Now he'd given her an engagement ring. Not exactly taking things slow, even when it was all pretend. He appreciated that she was still willing to uphold their arrangement, but he worried that one wrong move on his part would send her running.

Which was the last thing he wanted.

He opened the passenger-side door then walked around the front of the Audi, wishing he'd thought to bring her flowers or something—anything—that would have given him an excuse to linger at her place and have her all to himself.

The drive to the winery was only thirty minutes from Christine's place, and she spent most of it asking him about his week.

His shoulders relaxed as he shared progress on negotiating the merger of one of his firm's larger manufacturing clients with another company. He'd been focusing on cultivating the client relationship and on making sure they were abiding by all the local, state and federal laws that governed the industry. In turn, he asked her for her take on the continuing saga of Fortunado Real Estate's Austin branch. He'd talked to Maddie after she'd been back a few days, and his sister had seemed both frustrated and confused by the falloff in business.

Christine didn't have any more answers than his sister had but was clearly just as upset by the issues.

They arrived at the Mendoza Winery, situated in the picturesque landscape of the Texas hill country, and Gavin took Christine's hand as they approached the entrance.

"It's Schuyler's big show," she whispered, and her

words made him stop in his tracks. "What's wrong?" she asked as she turned to face him.

"I'm glad you're here with me tonight." He reached out and trailed a fingertip along her jaw. "Not because of our arrangement. It's more than that. You make me happy, Christine."

She hitched in a breath, and he could almost see the struggle as she tried to remain distant. He inwardly cheered when she went up on tiptoe to give him a quick kiss. "You make me happy, too," she said with an almost reluctant smile.

At this point he'd take reluctant. He'd take anything she was willing to give.

He glanced up as Schuyler called his name.

"Here we go," he whispered, and they continued toward the rustic yet modern lodge surrounded by acres of weathered grapevines. He hadn't been there since Schuyler's wedding and, once again, appreciated the beauty of what the Mendoza family had created.

Schuyler greeted Christine with a warm hug and a friendly chuck on the shoulder for Gavin. "You're late."

"I'm here now."

She rolled her eyes. "I bet the only reason is Christine."

"Maybe," he admitted.

"You would have skipped my reunion?" She glared at him, but he could see the sisterly amusement in her eyes.

"I would have made it eventually."

"Go on in." She waved them past her. "Our family's already here, along with Olivia and Alejandro." She glanced at Christine. "I wish I had a cheat sheet to give you for keeping all of the Fortunes straight. Olivia is one of Gerald Robinson's daughters. She and Alejandro Mendoza first met when he came to Austin from Miami for a wedding. They're pretty cute together." She checked her phone. "Nolan just texted. He and his brothers and sisters are on their way."

"Are his parents coming?" Gavin asked, thinking of his father.

Schuyler's mouth pinched into a thin line. "Their names are Miles and Sarah," she said quietly. "They didn't make the trip from New Orleans. Some kind of prior commitment, according to Nolan." She shook her head. "I don't think that's the truth."

"How did Dad respond?"

"He's taking it in stride. I think he's disappointed, but hopefully the Robinson siblings will show. That would help take his mind off Miles as well as the trouble with the agency. Apparently, Fortunado Real Estate isn't the only company having problems. Olivia told me her dad is stressed out because of some glitch with a processor manufactured by Robinson Tech. There's talk about a giant recall. It's as out of the blue as the trouble at the agency. I'm hoping this night will help everyone focus on more positive things."

"It's so nice that you put all of this together," Christine said. "Family is important, no matter how different the members of it might be."

"I couldn't agree more." Schuyler beamed. "I'm so glad you're here. We all are."

Gavin saw Christine's shoulders stiffen slightly, although not so much that Schuyler would notice. He knew what it meant and quickly ushered her into the winery.

"We're going to be okay," he told her in a hushed tone. "No one is going to get hurt in all of this."

She smiled but her eyes remained strained. "I know." Glancing around the interior of the winery, her features softened again. "It's gorgeous."

"Weren't you here for Schuyler's wedding last year?" It embarrassed him that he didn't remember, but surely she would have been invited? Christine was important to his family. She'd been a constant in their lives for a decade. The thought made guilt wash over him once again. Why hadn't he noticed her before now?

She shook her head. "I was invited but couldn't attend. My mom had a heart attack last spring so I spent a lot of time with her."

He stopped and stared down at her. "I didn't realize. She seems healthy now."

"She is," Christine said with a nod. "It's part of why she's so intent on the family dinners and all of us getting close. She's gotten a new lease on life."

"You have some explaining to do, son of mine."

At the sound of his mother's voice, he turned to see her approach, her arms held wide. "Hi, Mom." He bent to hug her, breathing in the familiar scent of the perfume she'd worn since he was a kid. "You look lovely."

"You look like you've been keeping secrets." She pulled away and wagged a finger at him. "I'll deal with that in a minute," she said, then turned to Christine. "First, let me say hello and congratulations to this beautiful girl."

"Hi, Barbara." Christine leaned in to hug his mother. "It's nice to see you."

"You, too, dear." Barbara took her hand. "Kenneth

tells me you're doing great things in Austin. He had such fun working with you last week."

"It seemed like old times," Christine admitted. "I'm surprised he was willing to hand the reins back over to Maddie and Zach without a fight."

Barbara laughed. "Don't let him fool you. He's loving every minute of retirement."

"Probably because he gets to spend more time with you," Christine said, and his mother looked pleased at the compliment.

Seriously, how was it that Christine hadn't been snatched up before now? Beautiful, sweet, smart and possessing one of the kindest hearts he'd ever met. Some man was going to be lucky to have her as his wife.

The thought that it wouldn't be him made Gavin's stomach turn like he'd just eaten food that had gone bad. But he knew she deserved someone better. Someone who could give her the kind of devotion she deserved.

"Speaking of spending time with people…" His mother turned her knowing gaze back to him. "Why was this relationship kept a secret?"

Gavin opened his mouth to answer, but Christine placed a hand on his. "It was my decision," she told his mother. "I wanted a chance for us to get to know each other—just the two of us—before we shared it with the family."

His mom smiled. "We can be a bit much."

"In the best way possible," Christine said, and Barbara gave her another hug.

"We're thrilled for both of you," his mom said. She held up Christine's hand. "It's a beautiful ring, lovely and classic just like the woman wearing it. I hope this means—"

"Mom." Gavin grimaced. "Please don't give us pressure about planning a quick wedding like Schuyler and Maddie have been. We're taking our time."

She took Gavin's hand and squeezed. "I was about to say I hope this means you'll be spending more time in Texas. And not that we're going to lose Christine to Colorado."

"I'm in Austin until the end of the month," he said, choosing not to directly answer the question. Of course, his mother already knew his plans for the next couple of weeks. But he wasn't about to address his future with Christine, not when his hold on her at the moment felt tenuous at best.

His mom inclined her head to study him before her attention was drawn to the front of the room. "Our New Orleans guests have arrived. I'm going to collect your father and go say hello."

Christine moved to his side as his mother crossed the room. "What is it about the Fortunes, legitimate or not, being so darn attractive? You have some mighty gorgeous genes in your family."

He chuckled despite the tension running through him. Each new leaf uncovered in the mess of a family tree Julius Fortune had planted added additional complications to all their lives. Of course, last year the Fortunado branch had been the ones complicating everything.

As Gavin watched his parents greet the new arrivals to this odd family reunion, he had to agree with Christine. Seven of the eight newcomers to the party were clearly related, he assumed, based on how they resembled each other, much the way he and his siblings looked alike.

He'd done a bit of research on Miles Fortune and his

New Orleans family. Nolan, who was the youngest son and a recent transplant to Austin, looked the most comfortable. Gavin guessed that had something to do with the woman on his arm, a brunette with long hair and a sweet smile. The rest of the group seemed hesitant to join the party, and Gavin didn't blame them. They were all making the best of a difficult situation.

"None of us got to meet Julius Fortune," he said tightly, "but by all accounts he was a sorry excuse for a man."

"Yes," Christine agreed, shifting closer so that the length of her body was pressed against him. Was it an unconscious move on her part or could she possibly know how much comfort he took in her nearness? "Despite that, his sons have good lives and from the looks of it, amazing families. I think that says something about all of you. If nothing else, remember you have that in common with your new relatives."

"Thank you," he whispered, placing an arm around her shoulder. "You make everything better."

She tipped up her chin to stare at him as if his words surprised her. He couldn't resist kissing her soft lips and didn't care that they might have an audience of his family, both new and old.

"Ah, young love," his brother Connor drawled as he gave Gavin a hearty slap on the back. "You two are damn adorable."

Gavin threw an elbow, but Connor dodged it with no problem. "And you're a pain in the—"

"Hi, Connor," Christine said, breaking apart from him.

His brother leaned in for a quick hug. "Hey, lovely lady. It's great to see you." He hitched a thumb in

Gavin's direction. "How did you get mixed up with this clown?"

"Just lucky, I guess," Christine answered, taking Connor's teasing in stride.

He winked. "Well, let me know if he gets out of line. I'd be honored to step in as your overprotective brother."

Gavin snorted. "You realize the two of us are actually related? What happened to you being too busy to come down for this?"

"Blood relations can't be helped," Connor answered. "And I wouldn't have missed this reunion. What do you think of the new crew?"

"I think we can all appreciate what they're going through, dealing with the knowledge of our shared family history." He shrugged. "I also think it's interesting that Dad's half brother isn't making an appearance tonight."

"I don't see any of the Robinsons here tonight, other than Olivia," Connor added. "I'm a little surprised at that. They've all seemed fairly open to this bizarre turn of events."

"I'm sure it's been tough with Gerald and Charlotte separating. Maybe that changes things for some of them? I couldn't imagine Mom and Dad ever breaking up."

"Thank heavens for that," Connor agreed. "I've heard that Charlotte hasn't taken the separation well."

"Can you blame her?" Christine asked, and Gavin realized there were things she didn't understand about the situation.

He shrugged. "Apparently, she knew about her husband's infidelities and kept some kind of a dossier on the illegitimate kids he'd sired."

Christine's big eyes widened. "That's awful."

"No doubt. I'm going to grab a drink then head over to introduce myself to the newcomers," Connor told them. "Can I get either of you something?"

"I'm fine for now," Christine responded.

Gavin shook his head. "Me, too."

When Connor walked away, she took Gavin's hand. "It means a lot to Schuyler that all of you are here." She glanced to where his sister and Carlo were talking to Nolan Fortune, tall and lean with dark brown hair. He held tightly to the hand of the woman at his side. "I think we should join them."

He nodded, unsure of why he felt so out of sorts or how to explain the way having Christine at his side soothed him. They approached the foursome, and Schuyler smiled gratefully.

"Let me introduce you both to my brother," she said. "This is Gavin and his fiancée, Christine Briscoe." She inclined her head toward the other couple. "Gavin, meet Nolan Fortune and *his* fiancée, Lizzie Sullivan."

"Thanks for coming tonight. I heard you've moved from New Orleans to Austin recently."

The man nodded, his brown eyes warm. "I'll always love NOLA, but my heart's in Texas so this is where I belong." He leaned in and dropped a gentle kiss on the top of Lizzie's head. "It's good that we all get together."

"I couldn't agree more," Gavin answered.

"Carlo and I are going to check on the food," Schuyler said. "If you or any of your siblings need anything, Nolan, just let me know."

"Will do." The man glanced around as Schuyler and Carlo walked away. "I think I could use a glass of the Mendoza wine I've heard so much about."

Gavin motioned to one of the servers holding a tray of wineglasses. "I can help with that."

Each of them took a glass of wine, and after thanking the server, Gavin lifted his glass. "A toast to new family and friendships. Sometimes the best endings come from the strangest starts."

Nolan and Lizzie shared a long look.

"I feel like we should ask how you two met," Christine said. "There's a story there."

Lizzie smiled. "It is a strange start," she admitted. "I saw Nolan playing in a jazz band in Austin the holiday season before last and we struck up a conversation from there."

Nolan draped an arm over his fiancée's shoulder. "But we didn't reconnect until this past December. I tried my best to mess things up, but she gave me another chance. Best moment of my life."

Gavin watched Christine's eyes light as she listened to the other couple. For all of her practicality, he realized she was a romantic at heart. And how had he honored that? With deals and arrangements, boundaries and timelines. What a fool he'd been.

"How about the two of you?" Lizzie took a slow sip of wine. "How did you meet?"

Gavin's stomach dipped as Christine's face fell for an instant before she flashed a too-bright smile. "We've known each other for years," she said airily. "It's the classic friends-first scenario."

"Friendship is key," Lizzie said, obviously sensing Christine's discomfort at being put on the spot.

"Actually…" Gavin leaned in, as if he was sharing a deep secret. "I'd had a crush on her for years."

"Who could blame you?" Nolan asked gamely.

"Exactly," Gavin agreed. "But I didn't think she'd ever go for a guy like me."

"He has a bit of a reputation," Christine offered, then added in a stage whisper, "As a *player.*"

"No." Lizzie patted a hand on her chest, feigning shock.

"But I knew I'd have to be a better man to earn my place at Christine's side." Gavin twirled the stem of the wineglass between two fingers, the truth of that statement hitting him like a Louisville Slugger to the chest. "So I…"

"You became one," Lizzie finished.

"Working on it," Gavin clarified.

"Most of us are a work in progress." Nolan lifted his glass to study the burgundy liquid inside. "This wine is fantastic."

Gavin was grateful his new relative was giving him an out on a subject that cut a little too close to home. "It's a private vintage. They only bring it out for special occasions."

"I'm sorry my dad wouldn't—" Nolan cleared his throat "—couldn't be here for this."

"I know my parents would love to meet him."

"What about the other brothers?"

Gavin felt his mouth drop open. "What other brothers?"

"You don't know about Gary and David?"

He shook his head.

Nolan ran a hand over his jaw. "Our fathers weren't Julius Fortune's only illegitimate sons. He had two more."

"I wondered about that," Schuyler said, rejoining the group. "I heard Ariana Lamonte—or I guess Fortune now—the reporter who married Jayden of the Paseo triplets, made a reference to there being 'others.'"

"Why didn't you say anything?" Gavin asked, his gut tightening once again.

"From what I could tell, the Paseo Fortunes were ambivalent about all of this. It was before Gerald and Deborah had reconciled so Jayden seemed to care more about protecting his mom from being hurt again than uncovering any more Fortunes. I think Ariana dropped it out of respect for Jayden's wishes."

"Our dad has known about his birth father for a while," Nolan revealed, leaning in closer to his fiancée. "He's done some research on his own over the years."

"Julius Fortune was a real piece of work," Gavin muttered.

"Quite true," Nolan agreed.

Schuyler shook her head. "We've got to stick together in all this. There's too much stressful stuff going on already and we can't let Julius's mistakes continue to haunt us. I only wish the rest of the Robinsons had been able to make it. They—"

As if on cue, Olivia hurried over to them. She held her cell phone in front of her like it was a poisonous snake. Glancing around wildly, her gaze settled on Schuyler.

"What's wrong?" Schuyler asked as Olivia took a shuddery breath.

Conversation in the lodge fell silent as everyone's attention focused on Olivia.

She swiped her hands across her cheeks. "A fire," she whispered. "Someone set fire to our family home. The Robinson estate has been destroyed."

Chapter Twelve

Christine registered the collective gasp that went up in the room at Olivia's words.

Schuyler wrapped her arms around the other woman's slim shoulders as the Fortunados and New Orleans Fortunes moved to surround them.

"What happened?" Kenneth asked, making his way through to the two women.

Olivia blinked several times as Schuyler released her. Alejandro Mendoza took his wife's hand, and Olivia leaned into him, clearly needing the support. Christine knew Olivia's courtship with Alejandro had been a whirlwind, and she'd even heard whispers that the engagement had been a sham at the beginning. Clearly, the two were soul mates and she couldn't help but wonder if she and Gavin might also have a happy ending to their strange beginning.

Olivia shook her head as Alejandro pulled her closer.

"We don't know exactly how it got started, but my brother Wes overheard the fire chief talking about suspected arson. Dad's the only one living at the estate at the moment, although Deborah is there quite a bit and each of us stops by when we can." She glanced at Schuyler. "We were all getting ready to come here. I think if someone did this purposefully, they must have known the estate would be empty tonight. In fact, things would have been worse except…" Her voice broke off as a sob escaped her lips.

"What is it?" Schuyler demanded. "Is everyone okay?"

Olivia shook her head. "I asked Ben to stop by the house and pick up a couple of photo albums. Apparently, he got there when the fire was really raging. He called 911 but tried to fight it on his own before the firefighters arrived. He—" She paused again, placing a hand over her mouth as she shook her head.

Christine automatically reached for Gavin's hand.

Kenneth placed a gentle hand on Olivia's arm. "Tell us," he whispered. "Is your brother okay?"

She gave a small shrug. "We don't know. He's on his way to the hospital. The EMTs tell us it's severe smoke inhalation." She dragged in a shuddering breath. "Alejandro and I need to leave. I have to get to the hospital—everyone's planning to stay there until we hear more about Ben. But I wanted you to understand…" She placed a hand to her cheek and shook her head. "I don't know what since none of this makes sense. The Fortune Robinsons would have been here, Schuyler. I promise."

"Of course. What do you need us to do?" Gavin's sister asked. "Please, Olivia. Let us help. We're your family, no matter how crazy the circumstances."

Olivia flashed a watery smile. "Would you go out

to the estate? It kills me that there's no one from the family there, but our priority is Ben. It's the house we all grew up in, and no matter what kind of problems Mom and Dad have been having recently, there are so many memories."

Although her parents' house didn't exactly fill Christine with sentimental thoughts, she thought about the Fortunados' stately home in Houston. She'd been to Kenneth and Barbara's home a number of times through the years and it had always struck her as such a happy place, as if the walls held on to the memories of children growing up there and of the bond among the Fortunado children. If the Robinson estate was anything like that, the loss of it would be far greater than simply physical property.

"Of course," Schuyler said and the entire room seemed to nod in unison.

"I've got to go," Olivia whispered.

"Do you need someone to drive the two of you?" Gavin asked, stepping forward. "With the shock and upset—"

"Thank you," Alejandro interrupted. "But we'll be fine."

Olivia nodded. "My family and I appreciate your willingness to help. We're grateful for each of you."

With that, she and Alejandro turned and walked out of the winery. There was a moment of heavy silence before the room exploded in shocked murmurs and muted conversations.

Gavin quickly grabbed a chair from a nearby table and climbed up. He shot Christine a grateful smile when she lifted two fingers to her mouth for a sharp whistle that drew everyone's attention to him.

"The fire at the Robinson estate is a tragic turn of

events," he began, "especially if the cause of the blaze turns out to be arson." He drew in a breath as if he felt the shocking possibility like a blow. "But the Fortune Robinsons need us now. All of us. We may not know each other well yet, but this is the time when we become one family."

Pride bloomed in Christine's chest as she glanced around to see all eyes riveted on Gavin as he spoke about the importance of solidarity and support. Even though most of his work was done in boardrooms with company leadership, she could imagine him in a courtroom, commanding the attention of judge and jury.

He tasked Valene and two of the New Orleans Fortunes—the oldest brother, Austin, and the baby of the family, Belle—with rounding up blankets, snack baskets, clean clothes and toiletry kits to take to the hospital for the Robinsons during the time they were keeping vigil for Ben. He asked Everett, his doctor brother, to head directly to the hospital to use his connections to facilitate whatever he could for the family. Schuyler volunteered to coordinate meals, and Maddie offered to secure a furnished rental house for Gerald Robinson and stock it with groceries and other household items before he got there.

Christine smiled and nodded as Gavin met her gaze across the sea of Fortunes. How was she supposed to do anything but fall in love with this man?

Oh. She placed a hand on her chest as panic washed through her. She was in love with Gavin. It was more than a crush or infatuation. So much for guarding her heart so she wouldn't be hurt at the end of this.

The knowledge that the end was inevitable did nothing to stem the tide of emotions she felt for him. The week of keeping her distance was forgotten like yesterday's news. After easing herself away from the group as Gavin mobilized everyone who was left to head to the estate, she hurried to the bathroom and splashed cold water on her face.

Nothing had changed about her outward appearance. She saw the same blue eyes and red hair holding its style thanks to a truckload of product, pale skin that looked a bit pastier than normal thanks to her panic-inducing revelation.

But inside her was a tumbling avalanche of doubt and fear. It was difficult to believe that her heart, which was so sure and full at the moment, could be in grave danger of shattering at the end of the month.

She took a few steadying breaths then headed back out.

Gavin waited in the dimly lit hallway.

"You don't have to do this," he said quietly, his face a stark mask.

Had he somehow read her mind? As if she had a choice on what her heart wanted—*who* her heart wanted. It had always been him.

She swallowed and tried to figure out how to explain her emotions to him without sending him running in the other direction. "I—"

He moved forward, taking her hands in his. "You've been great tonight. The best. But I know that it's overwhelming, all these Fortunes, and now the fire. It goes way beyond what you signed up for with us."

Did it ever, she thought.

"I can drop you at home before heading to the estate. I totally understand that you might not want to be a part of this mess. We're not your problem so—"

"Stop." She shook her head. He'd completely misread her reaction, but she couldn't blame him. She'd *tried* to pull away this week. Look where that had gotten her. "I'm going with you to the estate if you want me there."

"Of course," he answered without hesitation. The intensity of his gaze made her breath catch. "You've been the most amazing sport about all of this."

She choked out a laugh. So much for his devotion. A good sport? It was as if she could feel her heart splintering into a thousand pieces. She swallowed and tried not to let her emotions show. This was her chance. He'd given her an out. She should be smart and take it.

"It's all part of our deal," she answered with forced cheer.

His brows drew together, and he opened his mouth as if he wanted to argue with her assessment then snapped it shut again. "Are you ready?"

She nodded and followed him out of the winery. The only people left were servers, cleaning up the deserted party.

"You did an amazing job of rallying everyone," she told Gavin as they pulled away from the curb.

"We attorneys like to hear ourselves talk," he said with a wink.

"You do that too much."

He chuckled. "Talk?"

"Downplay the good things you do," she clarified and saw his knuckles tighten on the steering wheel. "Maddie told me you do pro-bono work with low-income families in the court system in Colorado."

"I've had a lot of success in my career. It's easy to give back in some small way."

"According to her, you devote a ton of hours to the cause."

"I have time on my hands when ski season ends."

"Gavin." She adjusted the seat belt strap so she could turn toward him. "This is what I'm talking about. I'm not sure why you want everyone to see you as this cavalier party guy, but it's a mask."

"Hiding my insightful thoughts and hidden depths."

"Yes," she answered simply. "You're a good man. I wish you could see yourself the way I do."

A muscle worked in his jaw as he accelerated onto the interstate. "I wish I could be the man you see," he said after several long minutes.

They drove the rest of the way to the Robinson estate in silence, although it was more comfortable than awkward. At some point Gavin reached across the front seat and laced her fingers with his. She was coming to expect the way he seemed to need to touch her as if she grounded him in the midst of the chaos swirling around them.

They exited the highway and drove through an upscale neighborhood of mansions. Christine gasped when the estate came into view. She hadn't seen the house in person before today, but given Gerald's success in the tech industry, she'd imagined it as spectacular.

It probably had been prior to today. But now she could only describe the scene in front of her as horrific. Fire trucks still lined the driveway, although the fire had been out long enough that the remains of the building were no longer smoking. The west section of the mansion, which clearly housed the garage, was still intact for the most part. As for the rest of the building, the walls that were left were no more than a blackened shell. Most of the structure was rubble and ash.

"Do you really think it was arson?" Christine asked as they parked behind Kenneth's Mercedes.

Gavin seemed as stunned by the scene as she felt. "I can't imagine who would do something like this. I've never heard rumblings that Gerald has any sworn enemies. If a person set a fire intent on doing this much damage, they must really hate him."

"It's unbelievable."

They got out of the SUV and joined the rest of the family who had assembled on the driveway in front of what should have been the front door.

"Has someone talked to the fire chief?" Gavin asked his dad.

"Not yet." Kenneth shook his head. "I think we're all paralyzed in the face of this much destruction. They're lucky Ben was the only one injured in the blaze. The level of damage blows my mind."

"I'll find him," Gavin said and jogged off in the direction of the row of fire trucks.

Barbara rested her head on her husband's shoulder. "It's awful but we both know home is where the heart is. Gerald and his family will survive this. He can rebuild and make new memories while holding on to the old."

Christine agreed, but that fact didn't make the devastation more palatable.

"I wonder if Charlotte knows," Connor murmured.

"I'm sure someone called her," Kenneth said. "Although I imagine she has everything of either sentimental or monetary value that belongs to her out of the house. I know Gerald wanted to make a clean break, especially after reconnecting with Deborah."

Gavin returned at that moment. "Normally they wouldn't allow access to the house so soon after firefighters got things under control. Apparently, Olivia told her dad we were coming out here. Gerald made some calls to ensure we'd be good. He has friends in high places. The chief says we can go in the areas they've deemed safe but to be careful of debris."

They each nodded.

"Let's split into groups," Gavin told them. "Connor and Savannah, you take some of us and start at the far end of the house nearest what's left of the garage. Mom and Dad, you take a group and start in the center and spread out. Christine and I will lead a crew to the far end of the rubble. I'm guessing that's where we'll find the master suite."

He gazed at what used to be the estate's main structure. "Look for clues as to what the room might have been used as and base your search for salvageable items there. As an example, you might find an appliance or two that tells you that room is the kitchen."

"What are we looking for?" Savannah asked, glancing over her shoulder toward the house.

"Anything of value, either financial or sentimental. Don't worry too much about pedigree or authenticity on any of the pieces we collect. This day is going to haunt the Robinson family, and I'd like them to know we were able to save something."

As his family and the Fortunes from New Orleans split up to tackle the first step in helping to heal their Robinson relatives, Gavin returned to Christine's side. She could see the tension around his mouth and eyes, feel the tension radiating from him.

"What if someone did this to my parents' house?" he asked softly. "It's unimaginable."

Once again she tamped down her doubts and wrapped her arms around his waist. "We're going to get them through this," she promised. "You're one family now. That matters."

He blew out a breath and kissed the top of her head. "You have no idea how glad I am that you're here with me."

"There's no place I'd rather be," she assured him, and together they followed his family into the wreckage.

Chapter Thirteen

It was almost midnight before Gavin walked Christine to the door of her condo.

"This was not the night I'd planned," he told her, rubbing a hand over his eyes.

They'd stayed at the Robinson estate until darkness made it dangerous to pick through the destruction. Although the house had been effectively torched, they'd managed to find a number of personal mementos that remained undamaged. They'd put the items into boxes and driven them to the rental house Maddie had secured.

It had seemed a sorry collection pushed into one corner of the empty garage, but Gavin hoped they'd bring some comfort to Gerald and the rest of the family.

They'd gone to grab dinner with Maddie, Zach, Schuyler, Carlo and Connor. Somehow Gavin needed the tangible reminder of his connection with his siblings. With everything going on from new Fortune revelations to the trouble with the family business to the fire, being able to laugh with his family was a balm to his soul. Had he been wishing for life as an only child just a couple of weeks ago? What a fool he'd been.

His family was a gift, just like this time with Christine. He'd taken both for granted. That was his problem and why he knew he had to let Christine go at the end of all this. He didn't have enough inside him to give her what she deserved.

"No one can plan for tragedy," she said, pulling a key ring out of her purse. "It's how a person handles it that shows what they're made of." She turned to him. "You were strong, articulate and compassionate tonight. It says so much about you as a person."

Damn. He wished he were a better man because walking away from Christine was going to hurt like hell.

"Right back at you," he said, then did a mental eye roll. He must have used up all his decent words earlier because he couldn't seem to form a coherent thought at the moment.

She unlocked the door and opened it to allow Princess Di onto the small porch. The dog's tail wagged enthusiastically as she greeted first Christine then Gavin with a head butt to the legs before trotting down the steps to do her business in the bushes.

"Do you need to walk her?" he asked, smiling at the dog. He really needed a pet. Maybe having something to come home to would help his outwardly exciting life feel not so lonely on the inside. "I could—"

"One of my neighbors took her out earlier." Christine

leaned inside and flipped on a light. "She'll be ready to hunker down for the night after her potty break."

"Right." Gavin rubbed a hand along the back of his neck. "I guess I should—"

"Would you like to come in for a bit?" she asked, almost hesitantly.

"Yes," he breathed, thanking the heavens for her invitation. It was ridiculous, this constant need to be with her. Reckless to allow himself to depend on her in any way. But he couldn't help himself. She was like a cool drink, and he'd been in the emotional desert of his own making for far too long.

She whistled for the dog, and Diana came loping back up the steps and into the house.

"Let's talk about your mad whistling skills," Gavin said as he closed the door behind them.

She grinned. "What can I say?" His insides tightened as a blush stained her cheeks when she added, "I'm good with my mouth."

If she'd smacked him over the head with a sledgehammer, he couldn't have been more shocked. He felt his mouth drop open, and desire pounded through him, flooding his veins with a sharp yearning.

Before he could get his muddled brain to form a response, she turned away. "Would you like a drink?" she asked over her shoulder. "A glass of water?"

"Sure." She toed out of her strappy heels and just that innocuous movement made another wave of need crash through him. Once again her pink-painted toes were the sexiest thing he'd ever seen.

She continued to the kitchen, hanging her purse over a chair. She took a dog biscuit from the cookie jar on the counter and then tossed it to Princess Di, who expertly caught it. The dog padded over to her bed while Christine pulled two glasses from an upper cabinet and filled them.

All the while he stood rooted in place, every cell in his body tingling with awareness and—Lord help them both—unbridled lust.

"Gavin?" She stared at him with wide eyes from the kitchen as if he were a hungry lion and she was the proverbial lamb invited to his feast. "I was joking about the mouth comment," she said with a hesitant laugh. "I went too far. I'm sorry."

Her apology jarred him from his lust-filled stupor. He ate up the distance between them in three long strides. "You never need to apologize," he said, cupping her face in his hands. "Yours is the most tantalizing mouth in the universe." He kissed her, nipping at the corner of her lips. "I thank my lucky stars each time you kiss me."

She moaned in the back of her throat as he ran his tongue along the seam of her lips. "Open for me," he whispered, and she did, her tongue mingling with his until his mind was swimming once more.

He ran his fingers through her hair, the way he'd been longing to all night, plucking out the thin pins that held the style in place.

At this moment he didn't give a damn that she was too good for him. He couldn't find it in himself to care about anything except the feel of her pressing into his chest. Her curves, her scent, the sweetness of her very essence.

Then she pulled away, and Gavin wanted to growl his protest. Was she going to send him away? Close herself off the way she had in the past week? He wasn't sure he could take that distance again.

"Why haven't we had sex?" she blurted, her eyes a little hazy but otherwise focused intently on his.

Just when he thought she couldn't surprise him anymore, another inadvertent blow sent him reeling.

"Um… I'm trying to respect you," he said, the words ringing false even to his own ears.

Her delicate brows drew together until she wasn't so much frowning as glaring at him. "You only sleep with women you don't respect?"

"No," he answered quickly. "I didn't mean that. What I'm trying to say is…" Oh, hell. What was he trying to say?

"You don't want me like that," she supplied and it took a moment for her words to register in his muddled mind. Right now the majority of his brain cells had gone on hiatus, allowing the lower half of him to take over the controls. That half wasn't exactly known for its good judgment.

"I want you in every way possible." He moved forward, and she stepped back as if putting distance between them was an unconscious response. No. He couldn't let her put up a wall between them. Not tonight.

He softened his tone and let his need for her flood his gaze. His career and the choices he'd made to keep himself closed off in his personal life had made him a master of the poker face.

He wondered if he'd ever been like Christine, whose beautiful emotions were written on her face.

"You agreed to help me because of the pressure from my family," he said slowly, needing the words to come out right. Knowing this moment mattered. "I don't want to take advantage of that…of you."

One side of her mouth kicked up. "What if I want to be taken advantage of?"

"Christine."

She studied him for a moment, and he could almost see the emotional war going on inside her. Which side would win out?

"I want you, Gavin."

He could have dropped to his knees in thanks. At the same time he didn't want her to have any doubts or regrets so he asked, "Are you sure?"

She took a step closer and wrapped her arms around his neck. "Never more sure," she promised and kissed him.

He let her set the pace and gave himself over to her slow, seductive torture. He couldn't remember the last time he'd been this happy, and it was all because of the beautiful woman in his arms.

More.

That was the refrain echoing in Christine's mind as she kissed Gavin. His hands reached up to stroke her bare shoulders, thumbs grazing over her collarbones. The featherlight touch made goose bumps break out along her skin, and all she could think was *more*.

She broke off the kiss, gratified when it took a few seconds for Gavin's gaze to focus on her. He'd given her the choice tonight, and she loved him for it. For so many reasons. Despite her doubts and the understanding that heartbreak was inevitable, she wanted this moment. This man.

Hitching in a breath, she pushed the suit coat off his shoulders and tossed it onto the counter. Gavin's nostrils flared as she moved closer and tugged on his tie, loosening the silk and sliding it from the collar.

"You can probably do this with more efficiency," she said, her voice husky as she started at the buttons of his shirt with shaky fingers.

"I like you undressing me," he whispered.

With every button, another inch of his muscled body was revealed. The shirtless Gavin she'd seen in photos from Fortunado beach vacations over the years didn't do justice to Gavin in the flesh. Heat radiated from him, and his skin felt soft yet firm under her touch.

When he'd shrugged out of the shirt, she took a moment to admire his body in a way she hadn't been able to the night of Diana's trip to the vet. Her girlie parts screamed to get on with things but she hushed them. This was every one of her fantasies come to life, and she had every intention of savoring the experience.

He gave her a sexy half smile. "I had no idea I could be so turned on just by how you look at me."

She reached out a hand and smoothed it up the hard planes of his chest. "How about when I do this?" she asked, wondering where in the world this confident seductress had been hiding.

Or perhaps not hiding. Maybe she'd simply been waiting for the right man to unlock her passion.

No doubt that Gavin held the key to everything.

"I love it."

She took her other hand and skimmed it across the front of his trousers, and she knew without a doubt he wanted her. He let out a soft groan as she cupped him then he encircled her wrist with one hand. "You're making me crazy, and I love it."

"It's an adventure," she told him, earning a low laugh.

"The best kind," he agreed, lifting her hand to his

shoulder. Then he reached around and unzipped the back of her dress. The silky fabric slid down her body and over her hips with ease, pooling at her feet.

Although inwardly cringing at standing in front of this perfect man in nothing but a black strapless bra and pair of lacy panties, Christine forced herself not to squirm. As she had minutes earlier with him, Gavin took his sweet time studying her, his chest rising and falling sharply as his gaze wandered along her body.

The need and desire she saw there gave her confidence, and for the first time she tried to see herself through Gavin's eyes. Clearly, he liked what he saw. Although she hadn't been overweight for over a decade, Christine still viewed herself through the lens of the chubby girl she'd once been. The misfit. The loser.

But she was a different woman now, and it was past time she start embracing who she'd become. She refused to allow herself to be stuck in her old insecurities.

Biting down on her lower lip, she reached around her back and unclasped the bra strap, tossing the thin piece of fabric to one side. Then she hooked her thumbs into the waistband of her panties and slid them down her hips.

All the while, Gavin's gaze remained on hers as his breathing grew more ragged.

"You have too many clothes on," she whispered.

"Damn straight," he agreed, his voice shaky.

He made quick work of his shoes and socks then unfastened his belt buckle and took off his pants, pushing them down his hips along with his boxers.

Suddenly, Christine had the realization that they were standing at the edge of her kitchen. Now what? She'd only been intimate with her previous boyfriend, and that had strictly been a lights out in the bedroom type of affair. Spontaneity was new for her, and while her body was a big fan, her brain wasn't quite sure how to deal with the reality of her new adventure. "Oh, my gosh."

Gavin chuckled. "I've gotten a lot of reactions in my day, but that's a new one."

"We're in the kitchen," she told him.

His grin widened, and he stepped forward. "You've never christened your kitchen?" he asked with a wink.

She shook her head.

He moved closer, reaching for her. "I like watching you try new things, and I have lots of them planned for tonight."

"You have a plan?" Her voice came out in a squeak.

"Do you trust me?" he whispered against her mouth, licking across the seam of her lips.

"Yes," she breathed.

"Good," he said and lifted her into his arms.

She gasped. The feel of his body was even more amazing than she could have imagined. Then she gasped again when her backside hit the smooth wood of the kitchen table.

Gavin trailed kisses along her jaw then down her neck and lower. He cupped her breasts in his big hands. When he took the tip of one, and then the other, into his mouth, she moaned from the pleasure of his mouth on her body. One hand moved lower, grazing her hips before gently pushing apart her legs and inching closer to her center.

She thought the attention to her breasts was enough to drive her mad with desire, but this was something else entirely. His fingers found a rhythm that had her craving more, the pressure in her body building with excruciating sweetness until she finally cried out. It felt as though a thousand stars were crashing over her, bathing her in a bright light that was like nothing she could have imagined.

Gavin kissed her, deep and slow, as the pulsing release subsided.

"I'll never look at this table the same way again," she whispered when he pulled away.

"I'm going to take that as a compliment," he answered with a husky chuckle.

"But you didn't..." Christine cleared her throat. "We aren't finished?"

"Not by a long shot." He gave her a sexy half smile that made her toes curl. Then he bent and took a wallet from his pants' pocket, pulling out a condom wrapper. "The next part of my master plan is moving to the bedroom."

"I like that plan."

She went to stand but before she could get to her feet, Gavin picked her up, one arm under her knees and the other cradling her back.

"Down the hall?"

She nodded. "You're pretty good with your hands," she told him, placing a hand on his bare chest. "But you haven't turned me into so much contented jelly that I can't walk."

"Pretty good?" He made a sound low in his throat. "That sounds like a challenge. And I could carry you for miles."

She bit down on the inside of her cheek when a denial popped to her lips. She might not feel confident about her body, thanks to years of being overweight, but she knew enough not to point out her flaws to Gavin.

He seemed as enthralled with her as she was with him, and that thought only served to open her heart to him even more.

"I can hear you thinking," he told her as he entered her bedroom.

She laughed softly as he tugged down the comforter and sheet and placed her on the mattress. "Then you'd better distract me."

"Exactly what I had in mind."

He opened the condom wrapper and, a moment later, skimmed his hands up her body until he was leveraging himself over her. She could feel him between her legs, but he held still as he smoothed his thumbs along the sides of her face, gazing into her eyes with an intensity that stole her breath.

"You're amazing," he whispered.

She automatically shook her head. Christine knew she was many things. Smart. Loyal. Dependable. Okay, that sounded more like she was describing her dog, but it was difficult to argue with the truth.

Gavin gripped her head and said again, "You. Are. Amazing."

Oh, no. She blinked several times. There was no way she was going to cry in front of him because he'd said something nice and she wanted desperately to believe him. She lifted her head and kissed him. Then he was inside her, moving in a rhythm that she knew was unique to the two of them. It was everything, and she still wanted more. Pressure built again, consuming her, but this time she wasn't alone in giving in to the pleasure. Gavin stayed with her, in her, until they lost themselves in the moment and all the things she felt but couldn't put into words.

And Christine knew the emotion…this night…this man…would change her life forever.

Chapter Fourteen

The next morning Gavin blinked awake, disoriented for a moment by his surroundings. The bedrooms at both his loft in Denver and the Driskill, where he was staying in downtown Austin, were decorated in a neutral color palette and dark wood furniture, so the pale blue walls and creamy white furniture he woke up to weren't what he expected.

The woman curled against him, still fast asleep, was another unexpected occurrence. Well, not exactly unexpected. He'd spent most of the night making love to Christine, which had been better than he ever could have imagined.

But Gavin didn't typically spend the night with the women he dated. More than typically. He didn't ever stay over an entire night. He also hadn't had a woman stay overnight with him since... Well, Christine's sleepover in his hotel room after Maddie's wedding had been the first.

It was part of his unwritten list of relationship rules not to complicate things. Simple was easier when it came to women, but Christine and their unorthodox arrangement were changing everything, especially his self-control.

He thought about sneaking out quietly but couldn't quite force himself to move. Her bright auburn hair was messy—thanks to him, most likely—and he loved how relaxed and unguarded she appeared in sleep.

Scratch that last bit. He liked it very much. Not loved. He wasn't a man who threw around the word *love* in any capacity with the women he dated. Dangerous territory that led to expectations he couldn't possibly meet.

Maybe that was why it was so easy to let down his guard with Christine. Their built-in end date was a safety net for his heart. So why did it feel like he was walking on an emotional tightrope with nothing but cold, hard ground beneath him as a landing?

He shifted away as a reality he wasn't willing to accept pummeled at his defenses, a tornado of doubts and long-held beliefs tearing at his walls.

Christine sighed then opened her eyes, her gaze soft and sleepy. Damn if he didn't want to pull her close, bury himself inside her and try to give her everything he'd never thought himself capable of offering a woman.

The mental reminder of his own shortcomings was enough to have him jerking away and climbing out of bed as if she'd just tried to bite him.

He was a damn coward.

She sat up, lifting the sheet to cover her beautiful breasts. Now that he knew firsthand the sweet taste of her skin and the way she fit with him, he had to force himself not to crawl under the covers again.

"Good morning," she said, and he hated himself for the doubt that clouded her eyes.

"Hi. I've got to go."

"Oh." The smile she gave him was shaky at best. "I understand."

She couldn't possibly because he was fumbling around with no playbook for this moment. Clearly, since he was making a complete mess of it. "I had fun last night," he said, even as he pulled on his trousers.

At some point during the night, he'd brought his clothes into the bedroom and put on boxers to sleep. Now he fastened his pants and reached for his shirt even as he shoved his feet into his loafers.

"Me, too," she said, tucking a loose strand of hair behind one ear. "Have you heard anything more about Ben or confirmation on the cause of the fire?"

Gavin glanced at his phone sitting on the nightstand. He hadn't even thought to touch the thing since she'd invited him in, so caught up in Christine as he was. He shook his head. "That's why I need to leave. I want to check on Ben."

She nodded, although the doubt remained in her gaze. "Let me know how he's doing. Maybe later we could—"

"I have a meeting tomorrow morning with a client and a presentation I need to finish. It's going to be a late Sunday in the office for me."

This time she didn't nod in agreement, and when her eyes narrowed as she studied him, a bead of sweat rolled down between his shoulder blades.

"Is there anything we need to talk about?" she asked,

and he could tell how hard she was working to keep her composure. He couldn't admire her or hate himself any more than he did at this moment.

"Nope," he lied.

"Right." She shifted to the edge of the bed, still holding the sheet up to cover her body. "I need to get dressed and take Di for a walk." When he didn't move, one delicate eyebrow arched. "Which means you should leave now."

Bam.

He thought he couldn't admire her more, until she went and gave attitude right back to him. Good for her. His Christine was stronger than she believed herself to be.

No. Not his. He was in the process of messing it up, because that was how he handled real intimacy.

He wasn't sure if it helped or made things worse to know he was an idiot.

With a sigh, he bent to kiss her goodbye. She turned her face at the last moment so his lips landed on her cheek.

"Have a nice rest of your day," she told him, refusing to make eye contact.

"I'll call you later," he promised.

"You can text me," she advised. "It's simpler that way."

Simple. Right. His new least favorite word in the English language.

"Have a good day," he said quietly. "And thank you again for last night…for everything. I—"

"It's fine, Gavin. We have an agreement. I get that. I hope you get positive news about Ben." With those polite words, she showed him that he was—without a doubt—the biggest jerk on the planet.

He didn't want to be. He didn't want this arrangement or the way she made him feel more than anyone ever had. But he couldn't find the words to make it better. Not when the hollowness inside his chest was a gaping pit that he couldn't seem to escape.

So he gave her a charming smile, even knowing she saw through that tired mask, and walked away.

"You look like hell."

As Gavin climbed in the passenger side of his brother's car, Everett studied him over the lenses of his mirrored sunglasses.

"Just drive," Gavin muttered, buckling the seat belt.

Everett chuckled and pulled away from the hotel's entrance. They were heading to the hospital to check in with the Robinson branch of the family. Gavin had spoken to Wes Fortune Robinson earlier. Ben's twin had reported that his brother was in stable condition but they were still monitoring him to ensure there was no additional injury to his lungs.

Gavin's sisters had taken care of the rental house for Gerald, as well as baskets of snacks at the hospital and a meal service for each of the Robinson siblings for the next week while they were still in the early days of processing the tragedy of their family home being burned to the ground.

Gavin couldn't imagine what they were going through, losing so many precious memories and family heirlooms. And all that on top of the troubles at Robinson Tech.

He still had trouble processing that the fire had been

ruled arson, as Wes had confirmed earlier. The tech industry might be cutthroat but who would have it in for Gerald so much that he or she would be willing to burn down the man's house? Couple that with the recall of one of their processors, and Gavin couldn't imagine things getting much worse for the tech company tycoon.

There was no doubt that Gerald had a crack legal team in-house or on retainer, but Gavin wanted to offer his help in whatever capacity was needed. Everett had offered to pick him up so they could drive over together. His brother had a friend on staff so he was monitoring Ben's recovery.

"Don't tell me you've already messed up things with Christine?" His brother gave a low chuckle even though Gavin didn't find any humor in the question.

"She's fine," he said through clenched teeth.

Everett shook his head and turned onto the boulevard that led to the hospital. "You messed it up. Did she dump you and give back that pretty rock she was wearing?"

"It's not like that."

"What's it like?"

How was he supposed to answer without lying? He'd been lying from the start, but his feelings for Christine didn't feel fake. Spending the night with her hadn't been part of their arrangement. The relationship was real and not real. And yes, he'd messed it up.

"I still don't get why everyone cares so much about my love life," he muttered.

"We want you to be happy." Everett gave him an annoyingly perceptive big-brother glance. "We love you, man."

Gavin pressed two fingers to his suddenly pounding

head. Christine made him happy. Could all his doubts and fears be wiped away by something so simple?

"I *am* happy." He felt like a broken record. "I've got a great life. My life is the envy of everyone around me."

"Are you trying to convince me or yourself?"

Gavin sucked in a breath but didn't respond.

"No one would have guessed you and Christine would be such a perfect match. On paper, you're two very different people."

"I don't care what other people think." Which wasn't true since the whole reason this had started was to appease his family.

"She's good for you," Everett said, ignoring Gavin's opinion.

"Yeah," he murmured. "She's amazing, which means she should be with someone who can appreciate and take care of her the way she deserves. I'm not a great bet when it comes to long-term."

"That doesn't have to be true."

"But it is," Gavin countered. "We both know it. Since I've been in Austin, I think every single member of this family has warned me about hurting her. There's a reason for that."

"We're not used to seeing you like this, but we believe you can make it work."

"Right."

"You can make it work, Gavin. Just stop being an idiot."

Gavin laughed softly. "Easier said than done."

"Maybe," Everett agreed. "The right woman makes it worth it. I can't imagine my life without Lila."

"Speaking of you and Lila..." Gavin arched a brow.

"Are you ready to talk about the new adventure you two are embarking on?"

Everett slanted him a look that answered the question without words. "You're more perceptive than you look. She wants to wait a few more weeks before announcing the pregnancy."

"I won't say a word." Gavin reached out a hand and squeezed his brother's shoulder. "But congratulations."

"Thanks." The smile Everett flashed was so full of love and happiness, it made Gavin's chest pinch. Would he ever feel that way? It was suddenly so easy to imagine a daughter with Christine's bright hair and sunny smile. But not if their relationship stayed in the pretend realm.

Everett pulled into the hospital parking lot a few minutes later. They weren't able to see Ben but they talked to Wes and Gerald. The police still had no suspects but the fire investigator had determined that the blaze originated in the master bedroom. It was strange, especially since Gerald hadn't been home at the time.

Although he didn't know the Robinsons well, Gavin still felt an overwhelming anger on their behalf toward whoever did this. It felt vindictive and personal. They needed to discover who was behind it. If an enemy was targeting Gerald Robinson, would they try something else or was destroying the family's home an isolated incident?

Gavin also had some things to work out in his own life. Namely his not-at-all-simple feelings for Christine. Was it as easy as Everett made it seem? Surely not. But he could manage it. All he had to do was talk to Christine and explain...

Explain what?

That he was terrified of hurting her. That he didn't believe he could make her happy. Neither would give her a reason to make their fake relationship real.

Scratch that. It was already real. Last night proved it. He could manage the rest. After all, it wasn't like he needed to drop to one knee.

He'd be going back to Denver at the end of next week. Why couldn't they have a long-distance relationship? He wasn't necessarily looking to have his cake and eat it, too, but why not?

Weekends and holidays together but enough separation that she wouldn't get the wrong idea about what he was able to give. They didn't have to be engaged. He might feel more for her than he had for a woman since...well, since ever. But that didn't change who he was at the core.

Why should it? He liked her. He had fun with her. Yet he didn't have to commit more than he could. At some point his family would give up with their insistence on seeing him settled. They'd understand he didn't have it in him. Surely, Christine would understand, as well.

He was an attorney, after all. He just needed to make his case to her.

Chapter Fifteen

Christine transferred a call to Maddie's office then continued entering data into the spreadsheet pulled up on the computer in front of her. Megan had called in sick, which was a bad habit the receptionist had on Monday mornings. They'd have to discuss expectations of the job, but for now Christine was filling in at the agency's front desk.

Two new clients, both looking for large family homes, had everyone feeling a bit more positive about the future. Maddie and Zach were both talented, dedicated Realtors, and Christine knew they'd find a way to overcome the recent setbacks.

She'd do everything she could to support them, even if it meant long hours and little rest. Staying busy was a good distraction from the tightness that had gripped her chest ever since Gavin's abrupt departure yesterday morning. As promised, he'd texted her last night, but she'd been too emotionally drained to respond with more than a few quick keystrokes.

They'd spent an amazing night together, but now she felt as unsure about his feelings as she had weeks ago. Did he still see her as a friend doing him a favor? The phrase "friends with benefits" came to mind, causing pain to slice across her stomach. That wasn't what she wanted from Gavin…from any man. Christine wasn't built for a casual fling and mentally kicked herself for believing it was more.

Needing a short break to clear her head, she popped over to Facebook. A sidebar advertisement for a popular Hill Country wedding venue on the screen, and she couldn't help but click on the link.

A moment later she sighed as she looked through the slideshow of charming, rustic wedding snapshots. The couples looked so happy, and she could clearly imagine futures of babies, family holidays and years filled with both laughter and tears. Not that her biological clock was exactly ticking at the moment, but she wanted to marry and have a family one day. It wasn't difficult to picture children with blond hair running through a backyard or cuddling up with a mini version of Gavin to read a bedtime story.

"Oh. My. God."

She started as Molly hovered over her shoulder.

Christine clicked the mouse, wanting to navigate away from the jeweler's website, but the young Realtor swatted at her hand.

"You're making plans," she said, excitement clear in her tone. "You and Gavin are really getting married. April is the perfect month for a wedding. It's not hot as an oven yet, and the bluebonnets will be blooming."

Christine shook her head. "I told you we want a long engagement not—"

"Did you say an April wedding?" Jenna joined them, leaning over the reception desk with wide eyes. "I bet Gavin will have a whole bunch of hot groomsmen."

"If Gavin's friends are half as hot as him, it's going to be the best weekend ever," Molly said with a laugh. "Christine, you are the luckiest woman on the planet."

"Why is Christine lucky?"

Jenna whirled around and Molly straightened as Gavin approached the desk. Christine lifted a hand to her cheek, knowing she must be blushing tomato-red. How much had he heard of her coworkers' ridiculous conversation?

"No reason," she told him, rising from the chair and straightening the hem of her silk blouse. "What are you doing here?"

"Come on, now." Molly grabbed Christine's arms and pushed her around the side of the desk. "Is that any way to greet your future bride? We were just talking about your April wedding. How many groomsmen are you planning to have? I'm just curious, you know?"

Christine squeezed shut her eyes for a quick moment and prayed for the floor to open up and swallow her whole. When everything remained the same, she glanced at Gavin with a shake of her head, mouthing "sorry."

To her utter shock, he seemed to take the whole situation in stride. He flashed his charming grin at first Molly and then Jenna. "Christine will make a beautiful spring bride."

The two women practically melted to the carpet even

as Christine felt her normally nonexistent temper rise to the surface.

"Molly," she said with a calm she didn't feel, "could you watch the phones for a minute? I'd like to talk to Gavin in private."

"Private," Molly repeated in a singsong voice. "I know what that's code for."

Christine gave her a withering stare. "No. You. Don't."

The woman's smile faded, and she slid into the receptionist's chair as if a teacher had just reprimanded her. "Take all the time you need," she said.

Jenna nodded. "I can help, too."

"Thank you. We'll be in my office." She raised an eyebrow in Gavin's direction, and when he winked, she thought she might feel steam coming out of her ears. She turned and stalked down the hall to her office.

"I like the sound of *private*," he said as he closed the door behind them.

"Are you out of your mind?" she demanded through clenched teeth. She wanted to scream the words, but the last thing she needed was Maddie or Valene, who was still in town from the weekend, running in to check on them.

"I don't think so." He took a step toward her, but she held up a hand, palm out.

"You let them believe we were getting married in three months."

Gavin was staring at her left hand, and she quickly pulled it to her side when she realized she was shaking.

"They seemed to be under that impression before I arrived on the scene."

"It was a mistake," she whispered, her cheeks growing hot again. "I was trying to correct it. We're supposed to be having a long engagement. Long enough that it will seem natural when it ends."

He shrugged. "What does the timing matter? It doesn't hurt anyone."

Me, she wanted to shout. *This whole thing is hurting me. Killing me.*

She drew in a deep breath. She would not break down in front of him. "What's going on between us?" she asked quietly.

He blinked then said, "We're friends."

Oh, gah. The friend zone. Was there anything worse?

"You're scheduled to return to Denver next week. What happens then?"

She held up her hand, the diamond flashing under the office's fluorescent lights. "What about this?"

"I've been thinking about that." He shoved his hands into his pockets and stared at a spot beyond her shoulder. "I know this thing started as a favor. You helping me out to distract my family."

She nodded and wished she'd never agreed to any of it.

"But we've had a ton of fun these past few weeks. It's been a blast."

A blast. A blast right through her heart.

"What are you saying, Gavin?"

He met her gaze then, but she couldn't read the expression in his eyes. He smiled, all easy charm, and it was like looking at a stranger.

"Austin's a quick flight to Denver. We can still hang out. Long weekends. Holidays. I come down to Texas often enough."

"So we'd keep dating?" Christine pressed a hand to

her chest. Somehow she thought she'd be overjoyed at his words. He didn't want their time together to end. But the ache in her heart grew deeper with every passing second.

"That's the plan. Of course we'd have to deal with the pretend engagement but—"

"You'd be my boyfriend?"

He lifted one hand and massaged the back of his neck. "If you want to put a label on it."

Her eyes narrowed, and he must have realized that was the wrong answer, because he flashed a sheepish smile. A "getting out of the dog house" smile.

"We spent the night together," she told him.

"It was wonderful," he agreed. "When I think about you in my arms, it makes me want—"

"Then you left," she interrupted, needing to keep this conversation on track. Even if she felt like the two of them were stuck on a runaway train heading for certain disaster. "You rushed out of there like I'd done something wrong."

"Not you, Christine. Never you." He shook his head. "But this arrangement started with me asking you to live a lie. I feel like I've taken advantage of you, and the fact that we slept together only makes it worse."

Ouch. Just when she thought the pain couldn't cut any deeper, Gavin managed it.

"I've got my life in Denver," he continued, running a hand through his hair. "You're here."

"A quick flight away," she muttered, repeating his words.

"I never imagined things would go this way. I care about you, more than I ever thought possible."

It was difficult to focus on his words over the roaring in her own ears. Christine had spent most of her life feeling like she wasn't enough. That she shouldn't expect too much. That scraps of affection or love with conditions placed on them were her lot in life.

Being with Gavin had changed that. She'd changed, and even if it meant losing him, she wasn't willing to go back to being the doormat she'd been before.

"I love you," she said quietly and the words felt right on her tongue. Based on the stricken look that crossed Gavin's face before he schooled his features, he hadn't been expecting her to say them. She tried for a smile, but it felt as if her cheeks were made of ice. "I didn't mean for it to happen. I didn't even want it to happen." She managed a hoarse laugh. "You're kind of irresistible."

"I'm not," he immediately countered.

"I wish that were the case," she told him. "Do you know I've had a crush on you forever?"

He shook his head, his jaw going slack.

"Yeah," she breathed. "So when you asked me to pose as your girlfriend—and then fiancée—for a few weeks, it was a no-brainer." She made a fist and gently knocked on the side of her head. "Turns out I should have thought it through a little more. I thought it would be a fun lark, you know? My chance with a guy so far out of my league it's like we aren't even playing the same sport."

"That's not true," he whispered.

"Which is exactly my problem," she admitted, crossing her arms over her chest. "Because you made me believe we had a chance. I lost sight of the lark part of things and began to believe what was happening between us was real."

"Christine, you have to understand—"

"Let me finish, Gavin. I need to say this, and you need to understand it." She pressed a hand to her hammering heart. "I'm more than I ever believed, and you helped me see that. I wish I could have gotten there on my own, but I'll be forever grateful for the gift you've given me. I know now that I deserve all my hopes and dreams coming true when it comes to love."

"You do."

"You deserve to believe in yourself, too."

He took a step back as if she'd hit him, then gave a startled laugh. "I don't think my self-esteem was ever in question."

"There's more to you than your career and your penchant for hurtling yourself down treacherous mountains or climbing sheer rock faces or any of the other extreme activities you do."

"I don't think so," he said with another hollow laugh. "All that extreme business keeps me pretty busy."

"You're a good man." She ignored his attempt to add levity to their conversation. "You have a big heart and a protective streak a mile long. You're dedicated and kind—"

"Tell that to the companies that I've managed to put out of business for the firm's clients."

"You have so much to give if you'd allow yourself to see it. I can imagine you as a husband and a father—"

He held up his hands. "Whoa, there."

But she wasn't finished. "I can imagine growing old with you and being at your side for whatever life brings. I don't want a casual, long-distance...whatever with you, Gavin. I want it all." She swiped at her cheeks when tears clouded her vision. "I *deserve* it all."

"Yes," he whispered then closed his eyes. When he opened them again, the emotion she'd seen there moments earlier had vanished, and she had to wonder if she'd imagined it in the first place. "But what if I'm not the man to give it to you?"

She drew in a breath and said the words that she'd never expected to utter. The words that broke her heart. "Then I'll find it with someone else."

Gavin stared at her as if he couldn't believe she'd be able to dismiss him so easily. But it wasn't easy. It felt as though she'd reached into her own chest to squeeze her heart until she could barely tolerate the pain. At the same time there was no doubt in her mind that she'd walk away if he couldn't give her what she wanted.

As hard as she'd fallen for him over these past few weeks, she'd also learned to value herself. She wanted to be with a man who could do the same, and while it might destroy her to have to accept Gavin wasn't that man, it was a chance she had to take.

"I don't know what to say," he admitted.

That simple statement made her shoulders sag. It seemed so obvious. She'd laid her heart out bare to him. He could cradle it in his arms or walk away and ignore her feelings or, worse, stomp all over her love for him. She hoped beyond hope that he'd choose her, that she hadn't misread or created in her own mind the deep emotion she saw in his green eyes.

"I think," she whispered, slipping the diamond ring from her finger and holding out to him, "that tells us both everything we need to know."

He stared at her for several long moments and then took the ring from her, shoving it into his pocket. She hated to see the pain in his gaze. Even though her own heart was breaking, it didn't give her any relief to know that Gavin was just as unhappy with this turn of events.

Still, she wouldn't compromise on what she knew she deserved. Not for him or anyone.

"You should probably go," she whispered, gesturing to her desk crowded with files. "I have a lot to get through this afternoon."

He gave a jerky nod but didn't leave. It was as if he was rooted in place, unable to move forward or back.

"Gavin, please. Don't make this harder on either of us."

"So it's the end?" he asked as if he couldn't quite believe it.

And she wasn't willing to cut him off entirely. It would be like chopping off her own arm. "For now. We'll still be friends…of a sort. Unless…"

He swayed toward her, pulled by an invisible thread. "Unless what?"

Her mouth felt like it was filled with sawdust. How was she supposed to answer? She'd told him she loved him, and he'd given her nothing in return. "I'm not sure," she admitted. "Maybe one of us will figure it out."

"Okay, then," he said, his tone hollow. "Goodbye, Christine. For now."

Then he turned and walked away.

Chapter Sixteen

Gavin drove around for hours after leaving Christine's office and eventually ended up on the highway, heading east toward Houston. He'd turned off his phone after five calls in a row from Maddie, four from Schuyler and one last call from Valene.

Obviously, word had gotten out that he and Christine were over. He still couldn't quite believe she'd…what? Broken up with him? Yes, they'd spent the past several weeks together but could it really be considered dating given how their relationship started?

His heart stuttered at the thought of losing her, offering a clear answer that his brain was trying to ignore.

She said she believed in him, told him she loved him, and somehow that honest admission had made every doubt and fear he'd ever had buzz through his veins like a swarm of angry bees.

It was one thing to be a part of her life within the

confines of their arrangement. Quite another to truly open himself up to her. He might be a success at plenty in his life, but he'd never been able to handle personal relationships for more than a short time.

His belief that he wasn't built for lasting love now felt like a cop-out. He could be fearless on the slopes or in his job but he was a coward when it counted.

The pain in her beautiful blue eyes had been like a knife to the chest. He wanted to be angry with her. They'd had a deal, and she'd gone and changed everything with her sweet honesty.

He turned up the radio, trying to drown out the voices in his head telling him he was an idiot. Two hours later he pulled into the long, winding driveway that led to his childhood home.

Once again he thought about the charred shell of the Robinson house. He couldn't imagine that kind of tragedy befalling his parents' home.

He parked and started up the walk to the front door, which opened before he'd made it to the top step.

"What a wonderful surprise," his mother said, opening her arms.

He enfolded her in a tight hug, probably taking more comfort from his mom's embrace than a grown man should. He was too emotionally spent to care.

"I wanted to see you before I head back to Denver."

She pulled away, patting his arms. "I thought you were in Austin until the end of next week?"

"I… Yeah…looks like I'm going to be leaving earlier than planned."

He followed her into the house as she glanced over her shoulder. "Any special reason?" she asked and something in her tone made him stop in his tracks.

"They got to you," he muttered.

"Who?"

"The trifecta of terror." When she didn't stop walking toward the kitchen, he trailed after her. "Otherwise known as my three sisters."

"Would you like a glass of tea?"

"Sure. Thanks."

"I made banana muffins this morning."

"Okay." He took a seat at the island, drumming his fingers against the cool marble countertop. "Which one of them called?"

"I spoke with Maddie about an hour ago," his mother admitted. "She was worried about you and wanted to know if you'd contacted your father or me."

"Does she know I'm here?"

Barbara pulled a glass from the cabinet then took a pitcher of iced tea out of the refrigerator. "I texted her when I saw you coming up the drive. All three of them were worried."

He snorted. "Doubtful. More likely they all wanted to lecture me on how badly I messed things up with Christine."

She set the glass of tea in front of him then took a glass container of muffins from the pantry and opened the lid. "From the look on your face, I don't think you need that lecture."

"Which wouldn't have stopped Maddie."

His mother inclined her head as if considering that. "You're right."

He plucked a muffin from the container and popped the whole thing into his mouth.

"Those are made for biting," his mother gently admonished.

He finished chewing and then swallowed. His mom was an excellent baker. "Gets to the same place either way."

She smiled. "Just like there are many paths to love."

"Wow," he murmured.

"Not the smoothest transition, I'll admit. But I assume you've driven all this way because you want to talk about your troubles."

He shook his head. "I want to eat muffins, drink iced tea and find a stupid action movie to watch on TV. I don't want to talk."

When Barbara said nothing in response, Gavin sighed. "Can I have another muffin first?"

"Bring it into the family room. We'll be more comfortable there."

He grabbed a muffin and his tea and then followed her into the wood-paneled family room. Dropping down on the overstuffed couch, he placed the glass on the coffee table and ate the muffin, again in one bite.

"It was all fake," he blurted, rubbing a hand across his eyes.

His mother's gentle gaze didn't waver. "Your relationship with Christine?"

"The engagement, the ring...everything." He nodded. "Schuyler was pushing me about my love life at Maddie's wedding, trying to set me up with every single woman she knew. It's been like that for a while. I'm not sure why everyone cares so much about me settling down, but I got sick of having people in my personal business. Who cares if I don't date seriously or stay single forever?"

"Your sisters want you to be happy," Barbara said.

Gavin leveled a look at her. "It's not just them. You

and Dad are the same way. No one believes I can manage my own happiness. I know you mean well, but it makes me crazy. Did you ever think that I'm just not cut out for a committed relationship?"

"Not once."

His chest constricted at her quiet confidence.

"You're wrong," he whispered. "Clearly. Just ask Christine."

"It doesn't sound as if your feelings for her are fake."

"Not now," he admitted. "I guess not even at the beginning. I always liked her…" He closed his eyes for a moment. "I'm embarrassed to admit I never really noticed her before Maddie's wedding. She was the nice girl who worked for Dad."

"She was more than that."

"Yes…well…" Condensation pooled around the lip of the iced tea glass, and he ran a finger across it before taking a long drink.

"Tell me how this fake yet not-so-fake relationship started."

"I lied to Schuyler at Maddie's reception. Told her I had a girlfriend so she'd stop with the matchmaking business."

"Did she stop?"

"She didn't believe me," he said, shaking his head.

"Your sister knows you well."

"Lucky me."

"True."

He felt the wisp of a smile curve his mouth. Neither his sisters nor his mother would let him get away with much, and he loved them for it. Mostly.

"She was pushing me on the identity of my mystery woman and why I hadn't brought her as my plus one.

I'd been dancing with Christine earlier in the night and told her how annoyed I was with the pressure to settle down. I'm not sure why, although I was grateful at the time, but she stepped in with Schuyler and claimed that *she* was my girlfriend."

"Schuyler believed that?"

His smile grew as he thought about Christine coming to his rescue that night. It had been refreshing, spontaneous and sexy as hell. "Christine is a great office manager, but she might have missed her calling with acting. She convinced Schuyler. She convinced *me*."

"Do you know she's always had a bit of a crush on you?"

"Not at the time." He frowned. "How did you?"

"Oh, sweetie. It's a mother's job to understand those kinds of things. That's part of the reason it made me happy to hear you two were together. She's got such a good heart, and you deserve someone like that."

"I don't," he whispered. "I hurt her, Mom."

"Because your feelings weren't the same as hers? I saw the two of you together. It didn't look fake." She leaned forward on her elbows. "No offense, son, but you aren't an actor."

"I cared…" He paused then said, "I *care* about her. I didn't expect it and things would have been so much easier if we'd stuck to the plan of having fun while I was in Austin. The engagement raised the stakes even more. Then it became more. I even suggested that we keep seeing each other after I go back to Denver."

"Where's the problem?"

"She told me she loved me." His body went tight as he waited for his mom's response.

"How dare she," Barbara murmured.

"Exactly."

His mother reached over and gave him a soft swat to the side of the head.

"What was that for?"

"Maybe I'm hoping to knock some sense into you. An amazing woman said she loves you and that's bad?"

"It means she has expectations," he said, then cringed.

"And?"

"I've never been great with that. I don't date seriously. I'm not built for it. Why can't anyone understand that?"

She held up her hand and ticked off responses on her fingers. "One, because it's not true. Two, because it's a weak excuse. Three, because you love her, too."

He automatically shook his head. "I don't. I can't."

"Gavin."

"Mom, every woman I've ever dated has told me I'm not husband material. I'm perfect for a good time, a few laughs and fun weekends away. I don't stick."

"They were wrong."

"I've dated a *lot* of women," he said quietly, embarrassed at having this conversation with the woman who raised him but needing someone to understand just the same.

"I'm aware," she answered.

"I've messed up with plenty of them. Not on purpose but in the same way I ruined things with Christine."

"You only have to get it right once."

He shook his head. "I don't…" He closed his eyes and let the truth wash over him. "I love her," he whispered.

"Yes," his mother answered simply.

"But what if I hurt her and—" His lungs burned as he drew air in. "What if I'm not enough? What if I can't be the man she deserves? What if I end up with my heart broken?"

"My sweet boy," his mother whispered as if she was comforting a toddler with a skinned knee. "You are so brave and adventurous."

"No. I'm a spineless coward. When things got serious, I turned tail. She has no reason to give me another chance."

"She loves you."

As if that was reason enough.

"But—"

"Are you going to try to make it work? No one can force you. Not your sisters or me. The choice is yours, Gavin. How much do you love her?"

"With more of my heart than I even realized existed."

"What's the worst thing that could happen?"

He blinked as understanding dawned. "Giving up on this chance at happiness. I have to fight for her to take me back. If she doesn't, I'll respect her decision. But if I don't try, then I'm going to live the rest of my life regretting it."

"Can I give you a piece of advice?"

He laughed softly. "Isn't that what you've been doing this whole time in your subtle way?"

Barbara patted his hand. "Make it count. You're all about taking risks, and the stakes don't get any higher than when you're putting your heart on the line. Go big or go home."

"Really?"

"Would you ski down a bunny hill when the double black is there for the taking?"

He laughed. "You're comparing Christine to a ski slope?"

"I'm telling you not to hold back."

Okay. He could do that. His mother was right. He'd hurt Christine and now he had to convince her to try again. She deserved to have him risk everything.

He stood abruptly. "I've got to go."

"Back to Austin?"

"To Denver," he clarified, then held up a hand when his mother frowned. "Trust me. I'm going to make this count."

"I do trust you."

"Thanks, Mom. For everything." He gave her a quick hug, then headed for his car. His dad walked into the house just as Gavin was exiting.

"Gavin." His father's expression was stony. "We need to talk about—"

"I'm fixing it," he answered without breaking stride.

"Good luck, then," his dad called.

Gavin would definitely need it.

Christine checked her makeup in the compact mirror she kept in her desk drawer Thursday morning. Not bad, she thought, given that she'd spent most of the previous night in tears.

She hadn't heard from Gavin after he'd left her office on Monday, not that she'd expected to. Hoped, but not expected. The news of their breakup—if she could call it that—had spread like wildfire through the office. If she had to guess, she would have said that several curious ears had been pressed to the door of Christine's office to overhear the heartbreaking conversation.

She'd tried to play it off and had managed to hold herself together when Maddie came in and threatened revenge on her brother for being an idiot.

Christine had claimed ending the engagement was a mutual decision, and in a way it had been. She simply hadn't been willing to take the scraps of affection Gavin offered. Not when she loved him so deeply. It was his own fault. He'd been the one to help her see that she deserved more than she normally expected. Unfortunately, that newfound understanding made it impossible for her to accept anything less from him.

It was only when she'd gotten home and curled up on her couch in private that the heartbreak had truly washed over her. Princess Di had joined her on the sofa, shoving her snout into Christine and then climbing onto her lap. She'd wrapped her arms around the sweet dog and cried for far too long.

So for the past two days, her routine had been the same. Game face at the office then allowing her mask to crumble once she returned home.

Today she'd woken up with the equivalent of a broken heart hangover. It would have been nice to call in sick and curl in a ball on the couch with a carton of Häagen-Dazs and the TV tuned to some reality-television marathon. But she had to pull herself together. So she'd applied makeup, slipped into her favorite dress and then headed for the office. She'd stopped to buy a dozen do-nuts on the way in, hoping the offering of dough and sugar would somehow prove to her coworkers that she was moving on.

As if.

She shoved the mirror into a desk drawer and headed for the conference room. Maddie had called an all-staff meeting in order to go over the latest sales figures and strategies for salvaging their declining business.

All eyes turned to Christine as she entered the room.

"Am I late?" she asked, tucking her hair behind one ear.

"Right on time," Zach answered from his place near the projection screen at the front of the room.

When Christine went to slip into a chair near the door, Maddie, who stood next to Zach, gestured to her. "We've got a place for you up here."

"Okay," Christine agreed, hoping no one expected her to speak at the meeting. When she was seated, Maddie clasped her hands in front of her chest.

"Now that we're all here," she announced, "we've got a special presentation today. Could someone dim the lights?"

Christine frowned as she glanced around. No one else seemed surprised at how oddly the meeting was starting.

Maddie took the seat across from Christine and hit a button on the laptop that sat in front of her on the conference table.

A background of a tropical scene with the words, "Love is the Adventure" superimposed on top of it displayed on the wide screen.

"It doesn't matter to me where I am..."

Christine froze as Gavin spoke into the silence of the room.

"As long as I'm with you."

She darted a quick glance at Maddie, who grinned broadly as she hit the computer's keyboard. A digitally edited photo of Gavin and Christine appeared on the screen. She recognized the original photo—it had been taken at the Fortune family reunion. Gavin had an arm slung over Christine's shoulder, pulling her tight to his side. She was leaning in, her head resting on his shoulder, and they both were smiling broadly.

The happiness radiating from her in the photo was undeniable, and a fresh wave of pain stabbed at her heart. But what surprised her was that Gavin looked just as happy, at peace and content in a way she thought she'd imagined during their time together.

Instead of the background of the Mendoza Winery, it looked like they were standing in front of the Eiffel Tower.

"Whether we're traveling to the great cities of the world," he said, his tone both tender and deliberate, "or to a tropical beach…"

Maddie winked at Christine as she clicked a button on the keyboard. Christine couldn't help but smile as her face, along with Gavin's, appeared superimposed onto the bodies of people lounging on the beach. The next photo showed them skiing, and in the following one they were traversing the Great Wall of China. She laughed, as did many of her coworkers, as the photos became an unofficial "where in the world are Gavin and Christine" montage.

Gavin continued to narrate all the adventures they could have together, and hope bloomed in her chest like the first crocuses of spring pushing through hard ground. That was the life she wanted, filled with fun and adventure, and most of all with Gavin at her side for every moment of it.

When the original photo popped up on the screen once again, someone in the back of the room flipped on the lights. Christine's breath caught as Gavin came forward.

"But in the end," he said, pinning her with his gaze, "I don't care where we are or what we do as long as we're together. I thought I had things all figured out but you changed everything for me. You changed me."

She shook her head automatically. She was the one who'd changed over these past few weeks. How could he—

"I love you, Christine," he said softly as he came to stand in front of her chair. "I can't imagine my life without you. I don't want to be half in or to put any limits on us. I want it all. I want to be the man you deserve." He reached out a hand, and she placed her fingers in his, the warmth of his touch sending sparks shooting along her skin. It had only been a couple of days since she'd seen him, but she'd missed this like he'd been gone for months. When she'd heard through the office grapevine that he'd returned to Denver, she figured it was the end.

But now he was offering her a new beginning.

He pulled her to her feet and lifted her hand to his mouth, brushing a soft kiss across her knuckles. "You deserve to be loved for exactly who you are. You're beautiful inside and out, kind and generous, and you make everything in my life better." He squeezed her fingers. "You are my life."

"Oh," she breathed. She wasn't sure she could put together any actual words without bursting into tears.

"If you give me another chance," he continued, and she felt her eyes widen as he dropped to one knee, "I'll spend the rest of my life showing you how much you mean to me."

There was a collective gasp in the room as he took out a small black box, opening it to reveal the sparkling diamond solitaire she'd already come to think of as hers.

"I don't want to wait," he told her with a hopeful smile. "I can't imagine losing you and I promise I'll never give you a reason to doubt me again. I love you so damn much, Christine. Will you marry me?"

Words. She needed words. Around the galloping beat of her heart and the blood hammering through her brain, she managed to nod.

"Yes," she finally whispered, and Gavin let out a pent-up breath that told her he hadn't been confident in her answer. But she had no doubt she'd love this man forever.

"I love you," she said as he slipped the ring onto her finger. "I'll love you for all of my life, Gavin."

As he stood and kissed her, a cheer went up throughout the room. Christine only had eyes for Gavin. She knew her life would never be the same and she wouldn't have it any other way.

In the past month she'd discovered a strength in herself she hadn't known she possessed and a love with a man who made her happy in ways she could never have imagined. She planned to hold on tight for whatever adventure life brought her way.

Epilogue

"I touched a fish," Christine said with a wide smile. "You must be sick of hearing me say that, but I still can't quite believe it." She giggled. "I swam with fish in the ocean and I didn't drown. It was like I was the Little Mermaid. Everything was beautiful. I can't believe I missed out on that for so long."

Gavin leaned in for a quick kiss, tucking a loose strand of hair behind her ear. They sat on two lounge chairs at an exclusive resort outside Cancún, watching shades of pink and gold streak across the evening sky.

"I'm glad you enjoyed snorkeling," he said. "Are you ready for parasailing tomorrow?"

"I'm ready for anything with you," she confirmed, then placed a hand on her stomach. "But let's not talk about it or I might lose my nerve."

"You can do it," he told her, taking her hand as he leaned back in his chair. "I believe you can do anything."

She bit down on her lower lip as tears pricked the backs of her eyes. Would she ever get used to his unwavering support?

She watched the waves curling against the shoreline for several minutes, letting the sound of the surf relax her. "I still feel a little guilty leaving Austin when things are so tumultuous with the agency and the Fortunes."

Gavin squeezed her fingers. "We're here for the weekend, sweetheart. Maddie and Zach totally support you taking a couple of days off."

Christine nodded. Gavin had suggested the spontaneous trip to the beach over dinner with his family the evening after he'd proposed to her. Her first instinct had been to say no, but both Maddie and Kenneth, who'd driven over from Houston with Barbara for the impromptu celebration, had agreed it was a fantastic idea.

Schuyler had taken her on a quick tropical-vacation shopping spree since Christine's only bathing suit was one she'd owned since college.

Her new life would take some getting used to, but she wouldn't change a thing. Every day with Gavin would be an adventure, whether he was at her side as she conquered her fears or they were settling into a normal routine in Austin. Gavin seemed to enjoy being back in Texas, opening his law firm's Austin branch.

They'd already talked about finding a house together, and Christine had agreed to sublet her condo to her sister when they did. Her parents had been supportive and surprisingly excited for her when she'd shared the news of her engagement with them. Aimee hadn't said much but she'd shoved a wedding magazine toward Christine and mumbled that she'd marked the pages with "not hideous" bridesmaid dresses.

She hadn't bothered to reveal the details of how her relationship with Gavin had actually started. No one seemed to doubt his feelings for her. After years of feeling like she didn't fit, Christine had discovered that believing she was worthy of being treated with love and respect made all the difference. They had a long way to go to become the close-knit family her mother hoped for, but Christine actually believed they had a chance of getting there.

So much of that had to do with how she'd changed and grown in the past few weeks. She was becoming exactly who she was meant to be and felt more confident than ever. She credited Gavin for helping her to see herself in a different way.

"I don't think I've ever enjoyed the ocean like this," Gavin said, his thumb tracing small circles on the center of her palm.

"Come on," she chided. "You don't have to pretend like this is something new for you. I know you've been to beaches all over the world."

"Yes," he agreed slowly, "but I was always moving, looking for the next thrill. Now I'm content. You're the best adventure I can imagine, and I don't need anything else."

He tugged on her hand and scooted to one side of the cushioned chair. She moved next to him, resting her head on his chest as he wrapped his arms around her.

"Thank you," he said against the top of her head, "for seeing something in me that I couldn't see in myself. I love you, Christine."

"I love you, too," she whispered. The connection they shared meant everything to her, and she was excited for a lifetime of both big adventures and tiny moments with

Gavin. Her heart overflowed with happiness as they watched the sun dip below the horizon. Each day would be a new beginning and she'd cherish every single one.

* * * * *

Look for the next book in
The Fortunes of Texas:
The Lost Fortunes continuity,
Her Secret Texas Valentine
by Helen Lacey.

On sale February 2019, wherever
Harlequin books and ebooks are sold.

#1 *New York Times* bestselling author

LINDA LAEL MILLER

presents:

The next great contemporary read from Harlequin Special Edition author Brenda Harlen! A touching story about the magic of creating a family and developing romantic relationships.

The cutest threesome in Haven is still in diapers.

Opening Haven's first boutique hotel is Liam Gilmore's longtime dream come true, especially when he hires alluring Macy Clayton as manager. Good thing the single mother's already spoken for—by her adorable eight-month-old triplets! Because Liam isn't looking for forever after. Then why is the playboy rancher fantasizing about a future with Macy and her trio of tiny charmers?

Available January 15, wherever books are sold.

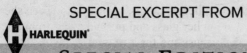
"You kissed me," he reminded her.

"The first time," she acknowledged.

"You kissed me back the second time."

"Has any woman ever not kissed you back?" she
wondered.

"I'm not interested in any other woman right now," he
told her. "I'm only interested in you."

The intensity of his gaze made her belly flutter. "I've
got three kids," she reminded him.

"That's not what's been holding me back."

"What's holding you back?"

"I'm trying to respect our working relationship."

"Yeah, that complicates things," she agreed. Then she finished the wine in her glass and pushed away from the table. "Will you excuse me for a minute? I just want to give my mom a call to check on the kids."

"Of course," he agreed. "But I can't promise the rest of that tart will be there when you get back."

She gave one last, lingering glance at the pastry before she said, "You can finish the tart."

He was tempted by the dessert, but he managed to resist. He didn't know how much longer he could hold out against his attraction to Macy—or if she wanted him to.

Had he crossed a line by flirting with her? She hadn't reacted in a way that suggested she was upset or offended, but she hadn't exactly flirted back, either.

"Is everything okay?" he asked when she returned to the table several minutes later.

She nodded. "I got caught in the middle of an argument."

"With your mom?"

"With myself."

His brows lifted. "Did you win?"

"I hope so," she said.

Then she set an antique key on the table and slid it toward him.

Don't miss
Claiming the Cowboy's Heart *by Brenda Harlen,*
available February 2019 wherever
Harlequin® Special Edition books and ebooks are sold.

www.Harlequin.com

Looking for more satisfying love stories
with community and family at their core?

Check out **Harlequin® Special Edition**
and **Love Inspired®** books!

New books available every month!

CONNECT WITH US AT:

Facebook.com/groups/HarlequinConnection

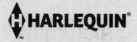

Facebook.com/HarlequinBooks

Twitter.com/HarlequinBooks

Instagram.com/HarlequinBooks

Pinterest.com/HarlequinBooks

ReaderService.com

HARLEQUIN®

**ROMANCE WHEN
YOU NEED IT**

HFGENRE2018

Love Harlequin romance?

DISCOVER.

Be the first to find out about promotions, news and exclusive content!

Facebook.com/HarlequinBooks

Twitter.com/HarlequinBooks

Instagram.com/HarlequinBooks

Pinterest.com/HarlequinBooks

ReaderService.com

EXPLORE.

Sign up for the Harlequin e-newsletter and download a free book from any series at **TryHarlequin.com.**

CONNECT.

Join our Harlequin community to share your thoughts and connect with other romance readers!
Facebook.com/groups/HarlequinConnection

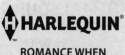

HARLEQUIN®

**ROMANCE WHEN
YOU NEED IT**

HSOCIAL2018